Percy Morgan wants to forget her past.

At the end of the first week, Percy sat cross-legged in the middle of her bed and brushed her hair. Most of the time, her long, coal-black hair was pulled tightly behind her head for it simply was not efficient to have it flowing around her shoulders while she cooked and cleaned. But she did not forget she had beautiful hair. She stroked it each night with slow, thorough, long movements that kept the hair thick and lustrous. Her father had had the same beautiful thick, wavy, black hair and the same fair complexion Percy had. She remembered standing beside him as a little girl, looking into a mirror and giggling at the resemblance. She had taken such pleasure in it in those days.

But that's as far as it goes, she told herself now. *I got your hair, Papa, but I don't have to have any of the rest of you. And I don't want any of the rest of you.*

Without getting up, she tossed her brush into the open trunk. The giggling little girl in the mirror was someone else—at least it felt that way sometimes—and those memories belonged to another lifetime. Percy Morgan no longer had the luxury of indulging in sentimental moments. Giggles were not only childish but irrelevant to real life, at least to the adult life into which she had grown.

SUSANNAH HAYDEN is the pen name of a versatile and gifted author of fiction and biography for both adults and children. Susannah makes her home in Colorado Springs with her husband and children.

Books by Susannah Hayden

HEARTSONG PRESENTS
HP14—A Matter of Choice
HP69—Between Love and Loyalty
HP77—The Road Before Me
HP113—Between the Memory and the Moment
HP117—Farther Along the Road
HP134—The Road Home
HP177—Nepali Noon
HP295—Tend the Light

Don't miss out on any of our super romances. Write to us at the following address for information on our newest releases and club information.

Heartsong Presents Readers' Service
PO Box 719
Uhrichsville, OH 44683

Light Beckons
the Dawn

Susannah Hayden

Heartsong Presents

For the people who have been beacons of God's light in my life.

A note from the author:
I love to hear from my readers! You may correspond with me by writing: **Susannah Hayden**
Author Relations
PO Box 719
Uhrichsville, OH 44683

ISBN 1-57748-750-8

LIGHT BECKONS THE DAWN

All Scripture quotations are taken from the Authorized King James Version of the Bible.

Cover illustration by Victoria Lisi and Julius.

PRINTED IN THE U.S.A.

one

Verdant, plush green gave way to the worn, well-trod trail. The meadow behind the lighthouse, speckled with rainbow-hued wildflowers, faded behind Joshua Wells as he nudged his sluggish gray mare toward the lumber camp. Although the miles between the lighthouse and the camp could be traversed in an hour by horseback, Josh felt as if he were moving across time, not mere landscape. As he left the lighthouse, he left more than sixty years of nineteenth-century heritage; as he neared the camp, he approached an unknown future that in less than two decades would take the northern Wisconsin peninsula into the twentieth century

For eight long years Josh had missed the journey. At seventeen, he had announced to his older sister, Lacey, who was running the Wells household during their mother's illness and father's consequent depression, that he was leaving to go away to school. All along he had insisted that he would come back to the isolated locale where they had been raised in the shadow of a lonely lighthouse, but no one had believed him because few people who left ever did. Josh's twenty-one-year-old twin brothers, Joel and Jeremiah, were nearly finished with college in Madison, and they were not coming back and no one had ever expected they would. But Joshua had always known that he would come back, no matter what anyone said. The lumber camp needed a doctor.

As the oldest son, Joshua bore the weight of expectation that he would become the next lighthouse keeper in the Wells family, a tradition maintained through three generations. But as a young teenager, Joshua embraced a different dream, and he went away in order to become a doctor. Joshua was convinced of the area's need for a doctor. He had seen many tragic lumber

5

accidents; and the small towns springing up along the shores of the northern peninsula were hours away from medical care. Now they had a doctor. His practice was small and erratic. Weeks might pass with everyone in good health and not more than a scratch to clean up, leaving Josh time to dream about the town that the camp might become or to pitch in with the physical labor of the lumberjacks. But, in the blink of an eye, all that could change and Josh would be entwined in emergency care where his years of training were exactly what was needed.

Today had been a slow one. With no pressing medical emergency demanding his time or expertise, Dr. Joshua Wells had been sent by his sister to check on their father, Daniel, and their youngest brother, Micah. Daniel Wells tended the lighthouse in which Lacey, Joshua, the twins, and Micah had been raised under the stern hand of their mother, Mary Wells. She had died shortly after Joshua left home. In Josh's mind, the stroke and debilitation that had taken her life were one more reason why the peninsula needed a doctor. After his wife's death, Daniel Wells had sunk into a spinning depression, but with time and Micah's burgeoning passion for the lighthouse, he had begun to function again. Daniel no longer sat in a chair, staring for hours at a time. He once again applied his spit-and-polish standards to the brass fixtures of the lighthouse and kept impeccable watch over the rocky waters in his charge. Meticulously, he taught Micah everything the sixteen-year-old boy would need to know to someday tend the lighthouse himself. But even after eight years, the light was still gone from Daniel's eyes and the spark missing from his step. Lacey insisted that she and Joshua must check on Daniel and Micah at least once a week, and she persistently counseled Micah to come to the lumber camp for help any time he thought their father was regressing.

After Mary's death, Lacey had stayed in the lighthouse with her brothers and father for as long as she could. But Travis Gates had at last finished building a home for her, and then he married her and carried her off to the lumber camp.

Many times since then she had crossed the miles back and forth, checking on Daniel and making sure her brothers completed their schooling under her tutelage. She was still supplying lesson plans and books for Micah. Joel and Jeremiah had done well enough to earn scholarships for college; Micah could go, too, but he did not want to.

Sixteen-year-old Micah Wells was a younger version of his father. The deer-specked meadow around the lighthouse thrilled him as much now as when he was seven years old, the solitude did not bother him, and Micah could not imagine his life anywhere else. Of the five Wells children, Micah alone still burned with a passion for the lighthouse, and he would be the fourth generation of Wellses to carry on the tradition of being an official lighthouse keeper. In his midfifties, Daniel still had many years before retirement, but Micah would be ready when the time came for him to assume the job.

Long before anything else, the lighthouse had been on the peninsula, standing regally at the peak of the cliff. For months at a time, it was inaccessible by water, especially in severe weather. The generations of Wellses who had lived there had long ago learned to conserve the goods brought to them by the supply boat, for they could never be sure when it would come again. In recent years better roads to the northern peninsula had been built; and with each passing year, even the path between the lighthouse and the expanding lumber camp was better defined.

Daniel Wells had been raised in the lighthouse; his siblings had left, but he had stayed and raised his family there. Now most of his children were gone; only Micah would stay and possibly produce another generation of Wells children in the old lighthouse.

As the lumber camp came into view, Joshua raised his eyes. He hated to call it a camp, for it was not really a camp anymore. It had one dirt street and a series of recently constructed permanent buildings. But it was not really a town, either. None of the permanent buildings would exist if it were not for the lumber industry thriving at the north end of the peninsula. As the cities in the southern part of the state grew and prospered, the demand for lumber increased. The thick, rich forest to the north seemed inexhaustible. Trees were milled into planks for homes and tables and chests and chairs and office buildings. But Joshua believed that the lumber camp would someday be much more than it was now. He could already see the progress that eight years had brought.

When in his teens, Joshua had worked as a lumberjack in the camp. He remembered the days when men slept in lean-to shelters and worked for weeks on end without decent food. Gradually buildings began to spring up, and the bunkhouses kept the men out of the elements. A cook arrived and demanded that the dining hall be enclosed and have a roaring fireplace at one end. The lumber camp manager, Tom Saget, dared to build a house and bring his wife and daughter to live in the camp. His daughter, Abby, had married Peter Regals, a lumberjack, and together they built another house. And Joshua had begun to see that the camp could become a town—that in fact the transformation was inevitable. The change was far from finished. But in his mind's eye, Joshua could see the finished picture: rows of homes, a church, a real school for his sister, Lacey, to teach in, a bank, mercantile shops—and a doctor's clinic.

While Joshua could not return to the lighthouse and be content there like his brother, Micah, he never regretted for a moment that he had come back to the peninsula. He had a natural talent for medicine, especially for the fast-thinking, quick-acting care needed in an emergency. When he finished his medical training, he had three job offers that would have given him a comfortable living in a civilized city, but he had turned them all down.

And then there was Priscilla, who had very nearly lured him away. His heart still twinged when he thought of her dark curls and shining eyes and the lilting laugh that enchanted everyone she met. She was a woman of far more depth than she let the world see: intelligent, articulate, opinionated, daring. But she would not come to the lumber camp to live, and Joshua could not do anything else but return. So last year they had parted sorrowfully, and Joshua had come home to his future.

Joshua was at the edge of the camp now, at one end of the single road that served as a center of social gatherings and business activities. The foreman's office stood prominently at the center of the cluster of buildings, while his home was at one end of the road. Across the way stood the dining hall, followed by a short row of houses and shedlike structures. Six bunkhouses were set back away from the road but with easy access to the dining hall. Completing the layout, at the far end of the road was a stable that housed the workhorses needed to haul the heavy lumber from the forest to the water, where it was floated south to a full-scale mill. Tom Saget who ran the lumber operation, also ran a small mill as a supplementary business to lumbering.

Josh was certain that mill operations would expand drastically before much longer. Soon the camp would have its own mill. Tom Saget, and his son-in-law, Peter Regals, had lobbied for years with the company that owned the lumber business. Machinery had been arriving for months, and soon the skilled workers to run the machines and mill the wood would come. And they would bring families, and they would need shops. Next would come the craftsmen, who could make furniture to ship all over the state. Excitement rose in Joshua's chest as he thought of what the future would bring.

"Hey, Josh!" a voice boomed and broke Joshua's reverie.

"Peter!" Josh called back. "What are you doing here? Don't you have work to do in the office?"

Peter grinned. "Lacey and Abby sent me out to wait for you."

"What Abby wants, Abby gets," Joshua said playfully.

Peter looked sheepish. "They wanted to be sure you came straight home."

Josh nodded. He slid off his horse and held the reins lightly as he fell into step with Peter. "I know. Lacey wants to know how Papa is. She always sends me to check on him, but she wants to be the judge of whether he is really all right."

Peter shrugged. "Can you blame her? After what she went through taking care of your mother while she was ill and then looking after Daniel when he could hardly put his shoes on for himself?"

Josh nodded again. "I know. And Micah is like her own son instead of her brother. But Papa and Micah are both doing fine. Don't you have to go back to the lumber office?"

Peter shook his head. "I'll finish my paperwork tonight."

"Does Tom know you're gone?"

Peter chuckled. "He indulges his daughter even more than I do."

"So there are some advantages to being married to the boss's daughter?"

"Only because I work hard and get the job done in my own way. I can't just count logs all day. I have to have time to dream."

"I know what you mean." Peter and Joshua had spent hours dreaming together before Josh left for school.

"I have some new drawings for you to see," Peter said. "I'll meet you at Lacey's house in a few minutes."

With a wave, Peter darted back to the office. Josh nodded with satisfaction, for seeing Peter's latest drawings of what the town might look like was always a treat.

two

When Joshua slung his lanky legs around the corner and into his sister's kitchen, Lacey Wells Gates raised an eyebrow at him. "You look more like Mama every day," Joshua said, laughing softly.

Lacey threw an enormous mound of biscuit dough down on the polished pine table. "That's not a bad thing. Now that I am a mother myself, I have a much greater appreciation for Mama's ways than I did when we were young," she said. She dug the heels of both hands into the dough and pushed with the automatic motion of years of kneading bread dough.

Joshua looked around. "Where are my adorable nephews, anyway?"

"Napping," Lacey answered, "and I want to make sure it stays that way."

Joshua lowered himself into a chair. He eyed the biscuit dough, unsure how long he would be able to restrain himself from pinching a bite. Mama had always disapproved of that habit. On the right day, Lacey would allow his indulgence, but his dilemma was that he was unsure of his sister's present mood.

"Adam is too old for naps, isn't he?" Josh asked. "Six-year-old boys don't take naps."

"They do when they don't feel well. He has nearly whined me out of my mind today."

"Maybe I should take a look at him." Joshua assumed his best doctoring expression.

"When he wakes up. If you go in there now, you'll wake up Caleb, too. And three-year-old boys do take naps."

"Yes, Mama, I mean, yes, ma'am."

Lacey swatted at her brother with a hand covered in flour.

Josh ducked and grinned.

"So?" Lacey said, kneading her dough.

"So, what?"

"So, how are Papa and Micah?"

Joshua shrugged. "Papa is Papa and Micah is Micah."

"What is that supposed to mean?"

"It means they are not any different than they were last week or than they will be next week. They're fine."

"Mama was fine one day and an invalid the next," Lacey reminded her brother.

"Come on, Lacey. You know that if anything like that happened to Papa, Micah would be over here lickety-split."

"It takes half an hour, even at a gallop. And what if you weren't here? What if you were off on one of your circuits to the towns?"

Joshua sighed. "They're fine, Lacey. Micah is as excited as ever about that old lighthouse, and it's good for Papa to be teaching Micah all he knows."

Lacey nodded and sighed. "You're right. Papa was so depressed for so long, I sometimes have a hard time believing that he's all right now."

"He still misses Mama, even after all these years, but he's so much better. I really don't think you need to worry as much as you do."

"Are they coming for supper?"

"I was supposed to invite them for supper?" Joshua asked innocently.

Lacey's eyes widened. Josh grinned.

"Yes, they're coming for supper. They won't be far behind me. Your biscuits won't be wasted on Micah. Papa says he eats like a horse now."

"He's a teenager. I can remember when Mama said the same thing about you. And she was right." Lacey folded over the dough and began to knead again.

"Peter said he would meet me over here with some new drawings," Josh said, changing the subject.

Lacey turned to stir the stew on the stove. "That's right. Abby and the kids are coming, too."

"For supper?"

Lacey nodded.

"No wonder you're making so many biscuits."

"A triple batch. I want some left over to pack in Travis's lunches. He spends nearly every day in the forest these days and doesn't make it home for lunch."

Joshua pinched a bit of dough and dropped it in his mouth. Lacey laughed. "I was wondering how long you could wait."

Chagrined, Josh avoided his sister's gaze and changed the subject. "Can't Travis eat the camp food when he's in the forest all day? I thought the men took lunch with them."

Lacey scowled. "He used to, until Lars Peterson got fed up and quit cooking. All the men are complaining about the food since he left. Now Travis would rather eat cold biscuits."

Suddenly, the back door swung open and a blond-headed ball of energy, about four feet high, whizzed past Lacey before she could stop him.

"Nathan, wait!" she called futilely. "The boys are sleeping!" With a groan, she reconciled herself to the fact that they would not be sleeping much longer.

Nathan's mother, Abby Regals, appeared in the doorway, breathless. Her five-year-old daughter, Francie, was attached to her skirt and moving in tiny steps; her eighteen-month-old boy, Nicholas, was squirming in her arms.

"I'm sorry, Lacey," Abby said plaintively. "He's over here so much he doesn't think he has to knock or be invited in. I just couldn't stop him from charging ahead of me."

"You know your children are like more of my own," Lacey said. She wiped her hands on a towel and reached to take Nicholas out of Abby's arms. He seemed fascinated by something on the ceiling and pointed and grunted persistently. Lacey tilted her head back, because she had no idea what was so interesting about the beams over their heads.

Abby gently tried to get Francie to let go of her skirt. The little girl loosened her grip enough to allow her mother to sit down and then put the child on her lap.

"How's Adam?" Abby asked.

"Still not himself," Lacey answered.

A crash and a wail from the room above them brought Joshua to his feet. "That's my cue," he said. "Dr. Josh will find out how Adam is." And he left.

Nicholas was through being held. "Down," he demanded, and Lacey complied. She set a fry pan on a throw rug and tried to interest him in that.

Abby smiled at the scene. "When we were little girls living miles apart, we were dying to see each other more often. It's hard to believe that we ended up living next door to each other in. . .in. . .in a lumber camp, of all places."

Lacey laughed. "We both swore we would never marry lumberjacks. We were going to get out of this place once and for all."

"Well, with two husbands and five children between us, it looks like we're pretty settled here."

"I don't know what I would do if you weren't here," Lacey said. "You and Peter forged the way when you built your home and stayed here."

"We have five homes now," Abby remarked. "And my parents are planning to add on again, you know."

"No, I didn't know. Why?"

Abby laughed. "I think they want some escape from the noise when the grandchildren come to visit."

"Peter and Travis have done a beautiful job with our homes," Lacey said, "but those two other homes are hardly more than shacks. I feel sorry for the wives who live in them."

"Bridget and Moriah don't have children yet," Abby said. "Their husbands are working hard, and those homes will be ready for families when the babies start to come along."

"At least we knew what we were getting into when we married lumberjacks and moved here," Lacey said. "Those poor women from the city. . .I can't imagine how they're coping. In the city they could have electric lights, even a telephone. They could go to church on Sundays and have ice delivered to their homes."

"You've never said you wanted all those things," Abby said.

"I don't. I'm used to life without them. But it's different for Bridget and Moriah."

"I talked to Bridget just the other day. She's doing very well but she's caught the virus."

"The virus? Is she sick?"

Abby laughed. "No, she's fine. I mean she's caught the one-day-we're-going-to-be-a-real-town virus."

"Oh, that," Lacey said, relieved. "Then I guess she'll be okay, after all. Speaking of the dreaded virus, I wonder where our husbands are. I understand Peter has new drawings."

"Yes, you'll love the sketch of the school this time. He wants it to have two rooms, not just one."

"Two rooms! He must be planning on a lot of students."

"He is. He's building for the future, not just what we need right now."

"Mama, I'm sick," a little voice said.

Lacey spun around to see six-year-old Adam standing in the doorway and looking droopy.

"I know you are, sweetheart," she said. "Did Uncle Josh come see you?"

The boy nodded. "He wanted me to open my mouth so he could look down my throat."

"So did you open your mouth?"

He shook his head emphatically. "My throat is private."

"It is?"

"Uh-huh. Uncle Josh shouldn't look at people's private places."

"Sweetheart, Uncle Josh is a doctor. We've talked about this before. You must let him look at your throat."

Again Adam shook his head. "Not going to."

Lacey sighed. "Then how about if you drink some tea with honey? Maybe that will make your throat feel better."

Now he nodded. Lacey turned and put the kettle on the stove. On the floor at her feet, Nicholas pounded the bottom of the frying pan with his open hand.

"He's going to break it, Mama," Adam said anxiously.

"No, I don't think he can break the pan," Lacey answered. She put some loose tea in a strainer and leaned against the counter to wait for the water to boil.

Francie finally slid off her mother's lap. "Where's Caleb?" she asked.

Lacey turned to Adam. "Is Caleb awake?"

Adam nodded.

"He's upstairs, Francie. You can go find him."

With her tiny steps, Francie moved slowly across the kitchen. When she had finally passed into the next room, Lacey turned to Abby. "How long has she been walking like that?"

"A few days. It takes me forever to go anywhere with her."

Lacey furrowed her brow. "Maybe Josh should have a look."

"I suppose it wouldn't hurt. But I think it's just a phase. Two weeks ago she skipped everywhere she went, and before that she rolled somersaults all over the house."

"It's probably nothing then." Lacey sank wearily into a chair. Nicholas scooted under the table, dragging the frying pan with him.

"Mama, I'm sick," Adam repeated.

"Yes, sweetheart, you are."

"I don't feel good."

"I know. Come here and sit on my lap."

He shook his head. "I'm not a baby."

Baby or not, he looked like he was ready to cry. Lacey patted her lap, but he refused to come.

The water boiled and Lacey got up to make tea. She put a generous helping of honey in it. Adam shuffled over and took a seat at the table. As Lacey set the tea in front of him, Joshua returned.

"How's the patient?" he asked.

"What's the diagnosis?" Lacey countered.

Joshua shrugged one shoulder. "That's a little difficult to say without a look at his throat. But he seems to have a slight fever."

Lacey nodded. "I thought so."

"Up! Up!" Nicholas demanded, and Joshua scooped him up off the floor.

"Uh-huh, Lacey, I think you'd better check the stew," Josh said.

Lacey flew across the kitchen, wooden spoon in hand. She peered over the bubbling pot and breathed with relief. "It's okay, but I'd better get back to the biscuits."

"Here, let me help," Abby said, snatching an apron off a hook next to the back door. Lacey produced a rolling pin and began to flatten the dough she had kneaded.

Joshua shook his head as he held the squirming Nicholas, who was now hanging upside down from his arms but did not want to be put down. "It's a wonder you ever get anything done," Joshua said, with sincere admiration. "This place is chaos."

"What's chaos?" Adam croaked.

"That means a place where everything seems out of control," Lacey explained quickly.

"I'm not out of control," Adam asserted.

"No, of course you're not," his mother agreed, as she rolled her eyes above his head at Abby and Josh.

Nicholas slid a little too far out of Joshua's arms and landed with a thud on his bottom. He squalled, stunned.

"Nicholas is out of control," Adam said.

three

The back door swung open once more, and the already busy kitchen got busier. Lacey's husband, Travis Gates, filled the doorway as he entered. Close behind him was Peter Regals, with a roll of wide papers neatly tucked under one arm.

Peter kissed Abby on the top of the head and stooped down to scoop up the wailing Nicholas all in one motion. Travis bent his dark head down to greet his weary wife with a kiss. Joshua watched as his sister's eyes met those of her husband. He could see the light that flashed between them. Both of them, weary from a long day, still spoke a wordless language that said they were glad to see each other. Peter and Abby looked at each other with similar expressions.

Josh looked from one couple to the other and felt afresh the pang in his heart—Priscilla. He tried to imagine her in this setting, a kitchen bursting with friends and family. She would have smiled at everyone, engaging the adults with her wit and charming the children with her playfulness. Everyone would like her; everyone always did. But Priscilla would not be doing what Lacey was doing—simmering stew, baking biscuits, and soothing a sick child all at one time, after having spent several hours teaching squirming children. The maid that Priscilla had had all her life would have dealt with the cooking and soothing, while a tutor handled the teaching. After a calm and civilized meal in the dining room, Priscilla would suggest a stroll through the streets. He had strolled the streets with her on many occasions. But here there were no streets to stroll, and the neighbors were all gathered in this house at the moment. No, Priscilla would not fit in here.

But who would fit in? The lumber camp was hardly the place to meet a prospective bride. Would he have to do what his father had done so long ago and venture to one of the cities to find a bride who would fit in at the camp better than Priscilla? Joshua had left the peninsula the first time in order to become a doctor. He had not thought much about marriage in those days. Meeting Priscilla had been quite accidental, and nearly two years had passed before he realized she regarded him as a prospective husband. He had allowed his own affection to grow guardedly, suspecting that he would be disappointed in the end—and he was.

Peter balanced Nicholas, who was now sucking his thumb and sobbing only intermittently, on his one hip and laid his roll of drawings on the table across from the mound of biscuit dough.

"No, no, no," Lacey protested as she scooped up the papers and thrust them back at Peter. "It's far too crowded in here. Take those drawings in the other room, please."

"We'll go to the dining room," Travis suggested.

Lacey shook her head. "Not there, either. I'll need to set the dining room table for supper soon. We won't all fit in here."

Travis sighed and smiled. "Is the living room floor all right?"

"Perfect." Lacey turned back to her biscuits. "As soon as Papa gets here, I'll bake these and we'll be ready to eat."

"Can I come?" Adam asked in his most pitiful voice.

Travis furrowed his brow and considered his son. "What's wrong with Adam?"

Lacey raised her eyebrows at Josh, who shook his head. "I can't be sure if he won't let me look in his throat."

"Adam?" Travis prodded gently.

Adam adamantly shook his head. "I don't want anyone to look at my throat. Can I see Uncle Peter's new pictures?"

Travis reached out his hand for his son, and together they trailed after Peter into the living room. Josh followed, also.

Peter squatted on the floor and unrolled his papers. The drawings of a small town had become familiar to everyone in the house, but each time Peter presented them for inspection, they had become a little more complex. Peter pictured a dozen small streets dotted with homes and a main road where the shops and offices would be. Adam snuggled under Peter's arm and put his face over the center of the map.

"I've thought about putting the school here," Peter said, pressing his finger into an intersection. "Lacey is already working hard with Nathan and Adam, and it won't be long before Francie and Caleb are ready for school, and then Nicholas."

Josh raised an eyebrow. "I'd like to see a school as much as anyone else, but we have only five children."

"We're planning for the future," Peter reminded him. "Someday there will be many more families with children living here. If we build the school first, they will be more likely to want to come here."

"You have a good point there, I suppose. If we want people to see we're a town, we have to look like one."

"Right," Travis agreed. "That's why we need a church, too."

"One thing at a time," Peter said. "For a while, the school might also be the church."

At the rap on the front door, Adam sprang up. "It's Grandpa!" He ran to the front door and heaved it open as quickly as an ill, scrawny six-year-old boy could. His grandfather's arms were waiting when he threw himself into them.

Daniel Wells lifted his oldest grandchild and pressed him against his chest. With his hand on Adam's cheek, he said, "You feel warm."

"I'm sick, but Uncle Joshua doesn't know what's wrong with me."

"What kind of doctor is he, then?" Daniel's eyes twinkled as he looked at his own son.

"I won't let him look at my throat," Adam declared proudly.

"That's not being fair, is it?" Daniel said.

Adam looked thoughtful, but he did not open his mouth for inspection.

Micah Wells followed his father into the room. Joshua looked on with pleasure at the young man his brother had become. As a child Adam's age, Micah had often tugged on Joshua's hand to pull him into the meadow behind their light-house home so they could look for deer and butterflies. Now, Micah had his father's broad shoulders and height, but he still had those sensitive blue eyes that were now being trained to scan the water swirling below the lighthouse for crafts in distress. Micah had the intensity to do the job well.

Micah pointed at the drawings. "Do you have something new?"

Peter pulled a sheet out from under the large map. "I've done a sketch of the building that would be a school and church. Here's the outside and here's what it might look like on the inside."

"Lacey should see this," Travis said. He turned his head toward the kitchen. "Lace!"

She appeared a moment later.

"Come see the school," Travis said.

Lacey kissed her father and waved at her brother, then squatted to inspect the drawings.

"I know I'm just an old man who lives in the lighthouse," Daniel Wells said, "but from what I hear whenever I come this way, not everyone is so keen on the idea of turning the camp into a town. They say that if they had wanted to live in a city and take a bath every week, they would have stayed in Milwaukee."

"I know who you're talking about, Daniel," Peter responded. "Troy Wilger makes a lot of noise, but there aren't so many men following him as he would like us to believe."

Travis agreed. "I think most of the men are in favor of developing the camp further. A lot of them came up here looking for work so they could save some money. But this is beautiful country up here. Why shouldn't they be able to settle here and raise families?"

"Well, you're a city boy and we managed to snag you," Daniel said. "So I guess there is hope that others will want to stay."

"It's inevitable," Peter insisted. "This area is too rich in natural resources not to attract people. Why shouldn't we plan for growth right from the start? We've already begun doing simple millwork here, and already we're more profitable. Travis's father is very close to closing a deal for a partnership with a major mill to move in here. And once the finished wood is more easily available up here, furniture makers and other craftsmen will be attracted to this area."

Lacey squinted at the drawing. "How many people will this building hold?"

"How many do you want it to hold?" Peter countered. "We could make it bigger."

"I couldn't begin to guess how many children we might have in a few years," Lacey said. "You're the one who has such a clear picture of the future."

"Don't forget your husband," Peter said. "Without the investment his father has already made here, we couldn't even think about next year, much less ten years."

Lacey smiled and nodded. Peter was right. Travis had come nine years ago on a secret scouting mission for his father. He had left temporarily to persuade his wealthy father to invest money for roads and basic mill equipment. And then he had come back to stay and build a future. Travis worked with Tom Saget, Abby's father, to carefully administer the generous investment his father had left in his hands. If the mill became successful, the senior Mr. Gates would more than make his money back.

"And then there's Josh," Travis said. "How many new towns can boast that they already have a doctor?"

Peter poked at the map. "And right here is where the new doctor's clinic is going to be."

Lacey gave a mock gasp. "You mean my brother is going to move out of my extra bedroom?"

Joshua eyed his sister. "When do we start building, Peter?"

"By midsummer," came the answer.

Joshua snapped his head around, surprised. "Really?"

"Really. I've organized a small crew, and we'll get that building up in no time. You'll have a waiting room and an exam room and a couple of rooms in the back to live in, just what you asked for."

"You're serious, aren't you?"

"Absolutely. After that, the school."

Lacey chuckled. "You might want to do something about the mess hall first. Old Lars left it in quite a jumble when he stomped off."

Peter and Travis shook their heads. "What got into him?" Peter asked. "How could a camp cook just up and leave one day between lunch and supper?"

"I don't know," Travis said. "But you're right. He left things in a mess. The new cook is not going to be happy."

"When does he come?" Joshua asked.

"Any day now," Travis responded. "His name is Percy Morgan."

"Is he any good?" Lacey asked.

"He doesn't have a lot of experience, but he comes with good references."

"Have you met him?"

Travis shook his head. "No. I didn't have time to go around looking for a cook. I hired him through the mail. I offered a three-month trial period. If he doesn't work out, we'll look again."

"Uncle Josh?" Adam said softly. He moved in a wilted way out of his grandfather's arms and toward his uncle. His face was flushed and his eyes bright.

"Yes, Adam?"

"You can look at my throat now."

four

Impatiently, Lacey Wells Gates waited for the water to boil. Another glance at the clock told her that her household would awaken soon—too soon. Lacey had hardly slept all night. Adam's flushed cheeks had turned into a full-fledged fever that left him thrashing in his bed and calling often for his mother. The cough had begun around midnight.

Not wanting him to disturb three-year-old Caleb, Lacey had taken her older son and settled him on a pallet on the dining room floor. The voice of motherly experience told her that it was pointless to go back upstairs to her own bed, so she had settled in beside her son and snatched a few minutes of sleep whenever he dozed off. Now she wanted the water to boil so she could have a cup of tea in peace before the family awoke and so the water would be ready when Adam needed another dose of tea and honey.

Joshua found his sister slumped at the kitchen table, waiting for the water to boil. "How is he?" Josh asked, his voice low to avoid waking the sleeping Adam in the next room.

Lacey raised her weary head. "He's been calmer the last couple of hours. Thank you for checking on him during the night."

"I didn't really do anything," Josh answered. "He needed his mother more than he needed a doctor."

"Still, it was reassuring to me to hear that you don't think this is a serious infection."

"I don't think it is," Josh answered guardedly, "but it's still important to keep him quiet. The best cure is rest. And keep Caleb away from him as much as possible."

Lacey sighed. "I'll try. But you know Caleb. He gets into everything he has a mind to get into."

Josh chuckled. "Your job is far harder than a lumberjack's!"

The kettle whistled at last, and Lacey got up to fix her tea. She turned her head at the sound of footsteps on the stairs.

Travis entered the kitchen and kissed his wife gently on the forehead. "I'll sit up with him tonight," he said softly.

"Do you want some breakfast?" she asked.

Travis shook his head. "I'll get something later."

"What will you get?" she challenged. "There's no camp cook."

"Matt Harden is doing his best with the breakfast duty these days," Travis said. "It will encourage him if I eat his food."

"Yes, it will encourage Matt," Joshua said, laughing, "but it may make you sick. The rumor is that you should stay away from his scrambled eggs."

"I'll keep that in mind," Travis answered. "Probably he hoards his eggs too long, trying to get enough to feed fifty men."

"He needs more chickens, but he keeps cooking the ones that lay the best."

"That reminds me," Lacey said, "Adam is too sick to feed our chickens."

"I'll do it," Travis assured her.

Outside, a horse whinnied and the wheels of a carriage clattered to a stop. The sound so common in a city area was almost unheard of on the northern peninsula.

Joshua raised an eyebrow. "Who is that, so early in the morning?"

Travis shrugged. "We'd better go see."

"If it's Micah, you let me know immediately," Lacey said sternly.

"Micah doesn't have a carriage," Joshua reminded his sister.

The horse whinnied again, this time more loudly.

Josh and Travis left the house and stepped into the broad, dusty street outside the house. A few men straggled out of the mess hall and wandered down the street, curious about the early morning intrusion on their routine.

A man in a frayed brown suit stepped down from a rickety carriage and absently looked around for a post to tie the horse to, but there was none. He then stooped to inspect the axle of his carriage.

Travis furrowed his brow. "I don't recognize the fellow," he said. "Do you?"

Josh shook his head. "Could it be the new cook?"

Travis's eyes brightened for a second, then narrowed. "There's a woman with him. Percy Morgan never said a word about bringing a wife."

"Does it really matter?" Joshua asked. "After all, we're trying to attract families."

"We don't have living quarters for a married couple," Travis reminded him.

"She could be his daughter," Josh speculated. "He seems quite a bit older than she is."

"We haven't got housing ready for a father and daughter, either," Travis said.

"I'm amazed that they got here in that carriage without breaking a wheel. The roads are rough."

From the height of the carriage, a young woman surveyed the growing crowd. She was dressed in a plain dark green dress and wore sturdy boots and a brown leather jacket. A broad-brimmed hat hid most of her features, but Josh could not help but notice the piercing black eyes.

"We'd better find out who they are," Josh said, and stepped toward the unlikely pair. He approached the carriage and extended his hand to the crouching man. "I'm Dr. Joshua Wells."

The man looked up sideways at Josh and did not stand to receive the welcome. "Nobody warned me about the roads up this way," he muttered.

"Most people come in on horseback or with a sturdy wagon," Josh said lightly. "We don't see too many carriages up here."

"I thought I heard the axle crack, but I guess it's all right."

Finally the man stood. He looked around. "This place is at the end of the world."

Josh was puzzled and glanced at Travis, who had joined him next to the carriage. "Surely you were warned what conditions were like," Josh said.

"Why would I be warned of anything?" the man asked.

"You are Percy Morgan, aren't you?" Travis asked.

"No. I'm not Percy Morgan, and apparently you don't know much about Percy Morgan."

Travis was taken aback. "We've not met. I hired Mr. Morgan through the mail to be our camp cook. We don't get many visitors here, so when you arrived, we assumed you were Mr. Morgan."

The man threw back his head and roared. He glanced up at the woman in the wagon. "You got them good, lady, I'll say that for you."

Josh and Travis glanced at each other, both agitated.

"Sir," Travis said, "if you are not Percy Morgan, perhaps you would give us the pleasure of introducing yourself."

The man shook his head. "It's not me you want to meet. I'm just the sucker who agreed to drive the lady all the way up here."

"The lady?" Josh said, turning to the woman in the carriage.

"That, my dear fellows, is Percy Morgan!" The man roared hilariously once again. He moved around to the back of the carriage and pulled on a trunk. With a smooth, experienced motion of visible exasperation, he heaved it off the carriage and dropped it. Dust swirled into a small cloud and quickly settled again. "And this, my friends, is all the worldly belongings of Miss Percy Morgan."

"Miss Percy Morgan?" Travis echoed faintly.

"You heard me," the man said. "Now if you don't mind, I'll be on my way. We drove most of the night through these back roads to get here. But from the looks of the place, I'm better off to turn around and go home now than look for any refreshment here."

Hearing her cue, Miss Percy Morgan stood up, stepped off the carriage, and landed lightly in the street. "Thank you, Mr. Booker. You've been most indulgent."

With laughter in his eyes, Mr. Booker looked at his customer. "I sure hope you know what you're doing, young lady." He swung himself up into the seat and snapped the reins of the horse. In another minute, he was gone.

Several dozen lumberjacks now stood in the street, staring at Miss Percy Morgan. Matt Harden emerged from the mess hall, spatula in hand.

"Travis, who is this and why is she here?" Matt demanded.

"Ah, Matt," Travis began awkwardly, "apparently your relief has arrived."

"What do you mean?" Matt barked.

"This is Percy Morgan," Travis answered. "The new cook."

"You never said the new cook was a girl," Matt said, scowling.

"I, ah, was unaware of that myself," Travis confessed, eyeing Percy Morgan. "You never mentioned that in our correspondence," he said to her softly.

"You never asked." She met Travis's gaze, daring him to question her further.

Her voice was firm and fierce, but Josh thought he heard a hint of fear embedded in arrogance. Percy Morgan took off her hat and shook free her long, wavy black hair. It fell across her shoulders, framing the creamy complexion of her face. Josh watched her shoulders rise and fall with her even, controlled breaths, as she held her head up straight and surveyed the gawking crowd.

"Travis Gates, you did this on purpose!" Troy Wilger pushed himself forward through the crowd. His ragged brown hair grew well past his shoulders and his beard had not been trimmed in months. His astonishment that the new cook was a woman evolved quickly into overt hostility. "This is all part of your plan to civilize us. You think you can bring a woman in here and make us all behave ourselves and mind our manners."

"Troy," Travis interjected, "I assure you I had no knowledge that—"

"Don't give me that!" Troy interrupted. "You don't make mistakes. Not like this."

"I wouldn't say it's a mistake," Travis defended himself, "perhaps just a misunderstanding. I'm sure we can work things out. Miss Morgan is very well qualified to cook for all of you."

"Do you mean you're going to let her stay?" Matt Harden challenged.

Travis forced himself to laugh. "I thought you were eager to be relieved of your culinary duties, Matt."

"I don't see how this can possibly work," Matt retorted. He waved his spatula in the air and turned his back.

"We won't know that unless we try," Travis insisted.

Josh's eyes were fixed on Percy Morgan. Her head never moved; her shoulders never twitched; her eyes never flinched. Her fingers held firmly the rim of her hat, and her feet stayed locked in place. *She has guts,* he told himself. *She really wants to do this.*

"She has to go," Troy Wilger shouted.

"We signed a contract," Travis said simply. "Three months' trial."

"Don't talk to me about contracts," Troy retorted. "This is a matter of integrity. She didn't tell you the truth about who she was."

"She answered all the questions I asked," Travis said. "And I promise you, her answers were quite satisfactory. Now perhaps one of you would help me with her trunk."

Troy thrust himself farther forward and lunged toward the trunk. "I'll help you, all right." With his powerful arms, he picked up the trunk and threw it toward Travis and Percy.

Instinctively, Joshua grabbed Percy's arm to pull her out of the trunk's trajectory, but she lost her balance and tumbled to the dirt. Indignant, she leaped to her feet and, as she did so, Josh heard the ripping sound. Although the trunk had not hit her, as Troy intended, it had landed on the edge of her skirt when she fell, and now her skirt had a huge rip along the bottom.

Josh jumped into action and pushed the trunk off of her garment, but the damage was done. The men in the street roared in amusement as Percy Morgan tried to fix her skirt, showing then the first hint of her being flustered since her arrival.

Troy Wilger, though, was not satisfied with her embarrassment and he lunged at Percy. This time Josh was not quick enough. Percy's slight frame was no match for Troy, and she tumbled backward, her head struck the side of the trunk, and everything went black.

five

Travis and Joshua hurled themselves at Troy Wilger and intercepted further assault on Percy. With his hands firmly planted on Troy's chest, Travis pushed, forcing the angry lumberjack to step backward or lose his balance.

"Miss Morgan!" Joshua dropped to his knees over the limp form of the newcomer. "Miss Morgan! Can you hear me?" Gently he slapped her cheek, but she gave no response. He put one hand under the back of her head, his fingers finding the slender nape of her neck.

"Is she all right?" Travis called over his shoulder.

"She's unconscious," Josh replied. Then he looked at his fingertips, damp and red. "And she's bleeding."

Matt Harden pushed his way past Travis and dropped his spatula in the dirt. "I'll help you move her," he said. "I may not think it's fitting for a woman to be camp cook, but she didn't deserve that."

"Take her to my house," Travis instructed.

Troy seemed to settle down. With a last disgusted look at Percy Morgan, he stomped off toward the mess hall.

"I'll deal with him later," Travis said, irritated. "What about Miss Morgan?"

"We'll take her home where she'll be out of further danger."

Matt moved toward Percy, but Joshua put his hand up to stop him. "Thank you, Matt, but I can manage."

"I want to help."

"Then get her trunk and take it to her room."

Joshua slipped one arm under Percy's shoulders and the other under her knees and easily stood up. *She hardly weighs anything.*

Travis fell into step beside him. "There's a cot on the back

31

porch," he told Joshua. "Lacey put it out there so Adam could rest in the afternoons."

"That will have to do," Joshua said. "I wish that clinic Peter has sketched were already built."

Moving quickly but smoothly, they retraced their steps to the Gates house and circled around to the sheltered back porch. Joshua laid Percy on the cot and reached for her limp wrist.

"Her pulse is a little fast, but regular," he announced, "and she seems to be breathing well."

Lacey appeared from the kitchen. "What happened out there?" she demanded.

"Troy Wilger and his gang," her husband answered, "and their usual barbarian behavior."

"And who is this?" Lacey asked, pointing at Percy.

"This is Percy Morgan," Travis answered.

"The cook you hired?"

"One and the same."

Lacey shook her head, a sly smile breaking on her lips. "You never mentioned that—"

"I didn't know," Travis said, cutting her off.

"I think we've established that Travis didn't know he was hiring a woman," Joshua said, "but she's here and she's hurt."

"I'm sorry, Josh. What do you need?" Lacey asked.

"A cool cloth and my medical bag."

"I'll get them," Travis said, and he disappeared into the house.

Lacey unfolded a quilt on the end of the cot and spread it over the still-unconscious Percy Morgan. The rosy color had drained from Percy's face, making her coal black hair appear even richer in tone. Her small features were smooth and well placed on her oval face.

"She's quite striking," Lacey observed. "I can imagine how Troy and his friends would feel about having a woman this attractive around."

Joshua did not answer. He took Percy's pulse again.

"On the other hand, you would think some of the men would be glad to have an attractive, unattached woman around. Things might be more interesting here for her than she imagined when she accepted the job."

Joshua glanced up. "What's taking Travis so long?"

"I'm here, I'm here." Travis came through the door and handed Josh a cool, damp cotton cloth.

Joshua gently pressed the cloth against the side of Percy's head, in the back under her black hair. Immediately he felt the warmth of the blood oozing into the cloth. He pressed on the wound with three fingers as he brushed away strands of hair to see what he was doing.

"What else do you need?" Lacey asked.

Joshua shook his head. "I'll be fine. The bleeding doesn't look too bad. If she doesn't come to soon, I'll use the smelling salts."

"I'd better go and see how the other men are taking the news," Travis said, "if there's nothing else I can do here."

Joshua nodded. "Go. We'll be fine."

"Mama!" came a plaintive cry from the kitchen.

"Is that Adam?" Joshua asked.

Lacey nodded. "His throat is worse."

"Just try to keep him quiet and comfortable. I'll look in on him later."

"Are you sure you don't need anything else?" Lacey asked, glancing over her shoulder at the kitchen door.

"No, she should wake up soon."

"Mama!"

"I'm coming, Adam," Lacey said, stepping toward the door.

Joshua repositioned the cloth. The bleeding seemed to be slowing.

Percy groaned and turned her head. "Where am I?" she asked as her eyes opened reluctantly and stared into the brown of Joshua's eyes.

Holding her gaze, he studied the size of her pupils. "You're going to be okay," Joshua said. "It's just a bump on the head and a small cut. The fact that you've regained consciousness so soon is a good sign."

"I have a headache bigger than the Civil War," Percy said, "but you didn't answer my question. Where am I?"

"You're on my sister's back porch, if you must know."

"Are you really a doctor?"

"Board certified."

"You have a sister?"

"Yes."

"And she has a back porch?"

"Yes, a small one." Josh was pleased that his patient appeared capable of sustaining coherent conversation.

"This doesn't sound like such an uncivilized place." Percy slowly moved her legs toward the side of the cot.

"I don't think you ought to move just yet," Joshua cautioned.

"But I want to," Percy answered.

"You just said your head hurt."

"It does. But it can't possibly hurt any more if I sit up." She had her legs over the side of the cot now and began to push her torso up. With a sigh, she leaned back against the side of the house and, after a moment, the view was in better focus. She looked out at the vegetable garden and henhouse. The scene was sharply different from the view of her old backyard. Although unfamiliar, it seemed oddly inviting. "It's a nice back porch."

"Here, let me change the cloth," Joshua said, taking away the blood-soaked cotton and replacing it with a clean rag.

"I guess that's why my head hurts so much," Percy said. She slipped her fingers in under his, took hold of the cloth, and nudged him away. "I can do this."

"Perhaps I failed to impress you with my assurance of board certification." His fingers still covered hers.

"I'm sure you're fully qualified. It's just that I'm not hurt all that badly."

Reluctantly, Joshua let go. "When it stops bleeding, I want to have a closer look at that gash."

Percy moved her head slowly from side to side. "I'm fine. Did I hear a child crying?"

"That's my nephew."

"So you have a sister and she has a back porch and a son."

"Two sons, actually."

"As I said, this doesn't sound like such an uncivilized place."

"I'm sorry that you got such an uncivilized welcome."

Percy scrunched up her forehead. "Why were they so angry? I'm a good cook. They'll see."

"It's a long story," Joshua said. "Don't take it personally."

Percy made a feeble attempt to laugh. "I am attacked within five minutes of arriving and you tell me not to take it personally?"

"I see your point. After you're here awhile, you'll understand better. Troy Wilger. . .well, he has his own ideas about how things should be done around here. It has nothing to do with you."

"Except that I'm a woman."

Joshua unrolled a bandage. "You represent change. Troy doesn't want change."

"But the camp needs a cook."

"Yes, it does. But you're not the kind of cook Troy had in mind."

"What did he have in mind?"

Joshua gently moved the hair off the base of her skull, exposing the wound. He inspected it thoughtfully. "I'll have to wrap that somehow," he said. "The wound is small. It should close within a couple of days."

"You're avoiding my question," Percy said. "What kind of cook did Troy have in mind?"

"Oh, somebody more rugged, a little rough around the edges, somebody who doesn't care for city ways."

"City ways? Up here?"

Joshua chuckled. "We're not all barbarians."

"No, of course not," Percy said, flushing. "After all, you are a real doctor."

"That's right. I even went to the city for training."

She looked around the porch. "You don't seem to have an office."

"I'm working on that," he said.

"I suppose that would be the city way to do things."

Joshua laughed aloud now. "Yes, it would. But I happen to be in favor of doctors having proper offices, with the right medicine and equipment."

"I thought this was just a lumber camp. Why does your sister with a back porch and two sons—and presumably a husband—live in a lumber camp?"

"That's a complicated question, but I suppose the simple answer is that she wants to."

"And you?"

"Me?"

"Surely you have other opportunities, better places to go."

Joshua shrugged. "If this is such a bad place to come to, why are you here?"

Percy hesitated ever so slightly. "Don't change the subject. Why do you live in a lumber camp? Why is there a house here?"

"We have several houses, actually, and several families."

"So this is not really a lumber camp?"

"Yes, it is. And no, it isn't."

Percy raised a questioning eyebrow.

"It has been a lumber camp. But it doesn't always have to be just that."

Percy nodded slowly. "I'm beginning to understand. Troy Wilger likes things the way they are, but not everyone does."

Joshua smiled. "Your deductive reasoning skills seem to be intact. I guess we can be sure that there's no permanent damage to your brain." He bent to examine the wound once more, pushing her thick, wavy hair away. Black, silky strands slipped through his fingers, and he had to hold her head more firmly. "Hold still now," he instructed, "and let me bandage this."

"I could do that," she insisted.

"Humor me," he responded. "Let me prove to you that I'm a real doctor."

The door from the kitchen creaked open, and Lacey stepped out onto the porch. "Oh, good, you're awake," Lacey said. "I'm Lacey Gates."

Percy could not turn her head to greet her hostess, but she said, "The sister with the back porch. Nice to meet you."

"Excuse me?" Lacey said, confused.

Josh chuckled but made no explanation to his sister. "That's right. And the older son is inside with a sore throat, and the presumed husband is trying to smooth things over with the men."

"Presumed husband? I assure you, my husband is quite real. I haven't the foggiest idea what you're talking about," Lacey said.

Josh caught the twinkle in Percy's eye and did not respond to his sister.

"The son with a sore throat is asking for Uncle Josh," Lacey said.

"I'll be in soon. I just want to get Miss Morgan settled."

six

"Your nephew needs you," Percy said as she stood up awkwardly. She had more of a headache than she wanted to admit. "Just point me in the direction of my trunk, please."

"Nonsense," Joshua protested. "When I said I wanted to get you settled, I meant I wanted you to be comfortable on this cot so you could rest. Perhaps later in the day we'll move you."

"I've intruded on your sister quite enough," Percy insisted. No matter what her welcome had been like, she was determined to make an impression of competence.

"You were unconscious for several minutes," Joshua reminded her. "I think it is premature for you to be up walking around."

"I'm perfectly fine. I have only the slightest headache remaining, and I'm sure a cup of tea will take care of that."

"Then let me fix you one. Lacey keeps a fine assortment."

Percy waived away his efforts. "I came here to run a kitchen. I'm sure I can manage a cup of tea."

Joshua sighed and snapped his medical bag shut. "Miss Morgan, are you always this stubborn?"

"Generally," she admitted. She had good reason for her stubborn streak, but she was not about to explain it to this stranger, no matter how sincere he was in taking care of her.

"What is the harm in letting someone look after you for a short while?"

"It's simply not necessary."

"If you're afraid of what the men may think if they hear you're hurt—"

"I'm not concerned in the least with what the men may think," Percy cut in. "It's simply not necessary for anyone to look after me at all. Now, please, be so kind as to direct me to my quarters."

"All right," Josh said in resignation. "But it's against my better judgment."

"Dr. Wells, please."

"Yes, yes, come this way. I'll walk you over."

"I told you that it is not necessary for you to coddle me. Just point."

"At least let me walk you to the front of the house. From there you can see where I'm pointing."

Percy marched down the steps of the porch and led the way around the side of the house, resisting the urge to clasp her aching head between her hands. From her new vantage point, she scanned the street. "I see where we came in," she said. "That must be the mess hall over there."

"Yes, it is," Josh confirmed. "There's a small room in the back. Your trunk should be waiting for you."

"Thank you, Dr. Wells."

"My name is Joshua." He hesitated. "I'm afraid the room is not much. It's quite small, and I don't know whether Travis had it cleaned out after the last cook left. The window doesn't open properly, and there's no lock on the door."

"Will I need a lock?" Percy asked sharply.

"I hope not," Josh answered softly. "But if you would like one installed, let me know."

Percy chuckled. "And you'll go right down to the hardware store and get one, won't you? I must have missed that shop on my tour of the city."

Josh laughed, too. "It might take a few weeks, but we could get one. And anything else you need—staples, kitchen supplies, pots. With enough time and patience, we can get whatever we need."

"I'll keep that in mind." She offered her hand to him firmly. "Thank you, Joshua Wells. I hope that someday I will have the opportunity to repay your kindness."

Josh shook her hand gently. "Thank you, Percy Morgan.

And if you need any more medical attention, you know where to find me."

She raised her eyebrows and looked around. "You can't go far."

"I do ride an occasional circuit to other places just as obscure as this one. But I'm not usually gone too long."

"Good day, then." She turned on one heel, lifted her skirt out of the dirt, and, with her head held high and her eyes straight ahead, she strutted across the street. The handful of men still standing in the street watched curiously, but no one spoke to her.

As Percy reached the mess hall, her heart was in her throat, but she was determined that the men staring at her would not unnerve her. She would ignore them until she felt ready to be in control of an encounter. With her lips pressed hard together, she pulled open the door to the mess hall and began to take stock of her new surroundings.

Travis Gates had told her by correspondence that the mess hall was a fairly new building. For years the men had eaten under a makeshift shelter, their fare prepared over an open fire, and this happened only seasonally. Gradually more and more men began to stay on the peninsula year round, and the lumbering continued as steadily as the harsh winter would allow. Travis had been instrumental in constructing an enclosed building that could house the men for meals and provide shelter and camaraderie when the weather kept them from working. This was the building that would be Percy Morgan's world, her workplace, her home.

Percy walked slowly through the dining area, admiring the craftsmanship of the tables. They were plain and functional, but beautiful in their simplicity and solidly built. The chairs, though of a half-dozen different designs, were just as well made. Percy had grown up in a home filled with fine furniture and she recognized craftsmanship when she saw it. Her mother would have been pleased to have a table and chairs of this quality in her home.

She came to the kitchen. No doubt Matt Harden had done his best to manage the unfamiliar territory, but he had left chaos in his wake. A greasy film covered everything in sight. Pots and dishes were stacked haphazardly around the room. The floor looked as if it had not been swept in three months. She would speak to Travis about the condition of the kitchen, Percy decided. She at least deserved to begin her work with reasonable conditions. Travis could assign a couple of the men to scrub down the kitchen and put things in order at her direction.

On the other hand, she told herself, some of the men were already inclined to throw her out. If she caused a stir about working conditions, they would find more reason to complain about her. She was here on a three-month trial basis and was determined to give Travis Gates no cause to exercise his option to let her go. No, she would have to tackle this job on her own. It would not be the first time she had taken on such a task, although she had learned these skills fairly recently.

Cautiously, she began to open cupboards and inspect the contents of the shelves. Flour, beans, lard, more flour, more beans. If she wanted to serve vegetables, she supposed she would have to grow them herself. She wondered if it was too late in the spring to put in a garden. And perhaps there was some dried meat hanging in a place she had not yet discovered. She would have to have something more than flour and beans to work with.

She hated to admit it, but her head was throbbing. In her trunk she had some chamomile tea, which would soothe her aching head and frazzled nerves. She also longed for a long, hot bath, but knew that that was out of the question and would be for as long as she stayed at the camp. Lugging the buckets of water, heating them, and filling a tub would be her own labor, not that of a servant. Percy did not suppose she would have time for such indulgence very often.

Percy pumped the handle above the sink, wondering if there really was water flowing straight into the kitchen.

Delightfully, there was! It was cold, clear, and sweet, apparently coming directly from a well. She splashed her face with her eyes wide open. Feeling momentarily refreshed, she looked around for a kettle or a pot clean enough in which to boil water. She found one that looked a little less dubious than most of the others, pumped some fresh water into it, and set it on the stove. The coals were still hot from breakfast, and the woodpile, though depleted, was nearby. Swiftly she stoked the wood and stirred up the fire. It would not take long for the water to heat.

Now she wondered where her small sleeping room might be. A narrow door off the kitchen looked likely. She pushed it open and peered in. The room was dim, even in the daylight, which puzzled Percy. Travis had obviously gone to great lengths to build a very workable kitchen—although dirty at the moment—and a pleasant dining hall. Why was the cook's room so disheartening? Percy stifled her self-pity with determination and took inventory of the room.

An oil lamp sat on the bedside table and she lit it. Even though it was midmorning and the sun was shining, she thought the light would help. Now she could see that a great shade tree stood right outside the window. Although it made the room dark, the shade surely kept it cool in the hot summer.

Joshua was right. It was small. The room held only a narrow bed that was hardly more than a cot, the small bedside table, a chair that had probably come from the dining room, and a row of hooks for clothing. It was at once clear that Percy would need to keep her trunk in the room for additional storage. Though her wardrobe was far from lavish, she had more than a pair of overalls to hang on a hook.

Her trunk had been placed with care along the only unoccupied wall in the room. Percy went to it now and opened it. She rummaged past the few books she owned—a Bible that had belonged to her grandmother, a book of poetry, and two novels—and felt between the layers of her clothing for the tin of chamomile tea. She sighed as she wondered if there was a cup clean enough to drink out of anywhere in the kitchen. Her head ached and she longed to lay it down on a soft, clean pillow. But of course she did not have a soft, clean pillow. In her determination to get the job, she had neglected to discuss with Travis what personal items she should bring with her. The bedding looked serviceable for the time being, but it would have to be washed before she would actually sleep in it. Perhaps she should have accepted Joshua Wells's invitation to spend the day on his sister's back porch. That might have given someone a chance to come over here and see the sad state of affairs.

No self-pity, Percy told herself sternly. She glanced down at her torn skirt. A skillful seamstress could probably mend the tear at least well enough to wear the garment for working in the kitchen. But Percy was not a skillful seamstress. She was fortunate to have learned to cook, and her own fetish for orderly surroundings dictated that she learn to clean. But she had never learned to sew.

Briefly she wondered whether Lacey Gates was handy with a needle and could perhaps mend the skirt. In the meantime, Percy decided she could at least change her clothes. She extracted a gray poplin skirt from her trunk and quickly traded it for the torn garment.

The water was boiling. Percy peered into the depths of a dark cup and decided it was safe to drink from it. She took the tea back to her room and sat on the edge of the bed. It was actually quite comfortable. Percy took her torn skirt and spread it out over the pillow. That would have to do until she felt up to scrubbing the bedding. She set the tea on the bedside table to steep and scooted back on the bed. Maybe Joshua was right; maybe she did need to rest a bit more. Her head beat like an African drum. She let her eyes close as she leaned her head back against the wall.

"Miss Morgan?" a voice called from the kitchen.

Percy scrambled to her feet, her head screaming with every

movement. She had not heard footsteps. "I'm here," she answered.

"I wonder if we might have a word."

It was Travis Gates. She recognized his voice from the encounter in the street that morning. If he had any notion of sending her away, he had another thing coming. They had signed a contract.

"I'm just settling in," Percy said as she stepped back into the kitchen. She regretted that she had not yet sipped her tea.

Travis smiled in a friendly way. She decided he was not there to send her away. At least not yet.

"I am sorry to disturb you," he said. "You've already had quite a morning."

"It's no trouble. What can I do for you?"

"I'm afraid I have some rather disturbing news."

So he was going to send her away!

"It's about supper," Travis continued. "Matt Harden refuses to prepare another meal. I explained to him your condition and that you were not likely ready to step in just yet, but he won't hear a word of it."

"Nonsense," Percy said emphatically. "I'm perfectly fine. The men need dinner and I'll cook it."

Travis nodded gratefully. "That would be very kind of you. And then perhaps we should have a more specific discussion about your duties."

"Yes, of course."

"Are the accommodations acceptable?"

"Yes, certainly."

"I looked in that room a few days ago." Travis smiled slyly. "I'll ask Lacey for some clean bedding and bring it over after lunch."

"That's not necessary."

"It's the least I can do after the welcome you received this morning."

"I'm quite fine."

"I'll see you after lunch, then."

Travis turned around and gingerly stepped across the sticky floor. Percy put a hand to her throbbing temple and decided that she needed that tea more than ever.

seven

A week passed. Percy had never been so tired in her whole life. She had personally scrubbed down the kitchen and dining hall from corner to corner on her hands and knees, breaking from the task only long enough to prepare three meals a day for the fifty or so lumberjacks. Her days began before dawn. She could make enormous batches of pancakes or biscuits in her sleep, and it often felt as if that was what she was doing. The men left for the work sites very early, and breakfast had to be ready precisely on time. She could spend two hours cooking, and fifty men would whiz through and inhale the meal in nine minutes or less. Someone would grab the crate of packed lunches, and Percy would be left with dishes and cleanup and a deadline for getting supper ready. At the end of the day, just when she was ready for stillness and quiet, the men would come in, ravenous and rowdy, and their boisterousness would send her spinning.

On the first day that she was alone with the monstrous kitchen, Joshua came by and he scowled when he found her on her knees, scraping crusted pancake batter from the floor. It was hard to tell how long it had been there, but its texture and color suggested a very long time. Percy had assured Josh that there were no lasting consequences to the incident in the street on her first morning and refused to allow him to check her bandage. It was not bleeding, her head had stopped hurting, and she had far too much to do to lie in bed as he might have liked her to do. After a few minutes of awkward conversation that never seemed to veer from the cut on her head, Joshua left, but his parting words were a stern warning not to overdo.

When Percy was alone again, she scraped at the pancake batter a little more slowly. She would have liked it if Joshua

Wells had stayed longer, but at the same time she knew she had driven him off with her impertinence.

At least three times every hour Percy admitted to herself that she ached and was tired and felt overwhelmed by what she had undertaken. But she was determined not to admit it to anyone else. She simply pressed on with the task of transforming the mess hall into an orderly, functioning state so that the next time Dr. Wells came by, he would see that everything was under control.

❧

One day Travis Gates came by to ask what supplies she needed. She gave him a list, grateful for his promise to get them as quickly as possible but knowing that it might still be several weeks. Her mind whirled with the challenge of providing some menu variety with the limited supplies on hand. She hoped for several hundred pounds of potatoes to arrive sooner rather than later.

Once she proved her industriousness by cleaning the mess hall without a whimper of complaint, she intended to approach Travis about having someone dig a garden where she could put in some vegetables. And the dozen scrawny hens in the coop behind the mess hall might provide enough eggs for pancakes or dessert cakes, but she dreamed of having enough to scramble eggs for breakfast twice a week.

Percy had noticed Lacey Gates and another young woman weeding a vegetable patch between two houses. It must have been the garden that Percy had seen from Lacey's back porch. Lacey and her companion seemed to converse pleasantly and easily as they worked, while their children of various ages roamed around, exploring the meadow and creek behind the short row of buildings. From a distance, Lacey Gates struck Percy as being competent and unflappable. Her children were as mischievous as any children, Percy supposed, but Lacey seemed to handle them with an admirable, gentle firmness. She worked in the garden swiftly and expertly, hung her tidy wash on Wednesday afternoon, and steered her children toward the kitchen with minimal resistance when it was time to prepare the evening meal. Her companion, whom Lacey judged to be about the same age as Lacey and a few years older than her own twenty-one years, seemed to hear a different drummer as Percy observed them in the street. She arrived at the vegetable patch after Lacey was already hard at work, and her wash was more likely to be laid out over the railing of her front porch. Even her children giggled and romped more energetically than the Gates boys. Despite their differences, the two women appeared clearly companionable.

Travis Gates had told her that there were two other young women, new brides who were lonely themselves, and hinted that it would not be as difficult as she imagined to find friendship in the camp. But Percy had not taken time to socialize with her new neighbors beyond returning Lacey's morning wave several times. As it was, she fell into bed each night exhausted by the day's labor. The thought of having to be polite and engaging with other civilized people overwhelmed her. Her mind was focused on the job she had come to do, and she had not expected to have friendships with other women at a lumber camp. Despite the clear availability of four other young women, Percy could not muster the energy to be sociable and so she made no attempt.

Dealing with the lumberjacks was another matter. She had to face the whole lot of them morning and evening, but nothing dictated that she had to be sociable. Every time Matt Harden came into the mess hall, he looked as if he wanted to say something, but he never did. She looked him in the eye and waited, but nothing came. After the first two days, Percy paid no attention. If he had something to say, he should just say it, she told herself. She was far too busy to try to urge it out of him. Troy Wilger glared at her each time he passed through the line and consistently found something critical to say about the food, generally in a very loud voice. But Percy could not help noticing that he came back for seconds more frequently than anyone else. She was sure she would please his appetite once she had a full range of staples available.

Most of the other men scrutinized her more silently. As they filled their plates at the serving table, their eyes were more often on her than the food. She refilled the platters as quickly as they emptied them. If anyone stared at her, she stared back fiercely and intently. Once Troy Wilger had caught her staring down a younger lumberjack and roared hilariously and within seconds the whole mess hall shook with laughter at the standoff. Percy blushed with fury but did not break her glare. Finally, the man moved on through the line. The laughter heightened, but this time the young man blushed. After that he did not look Percy in the eye again, and not many others did, either.

At the end of the first week, Percy sat cross-legged in the middle of her bed and brushed her hair. Most of the time, her long, coal black hair was pulled tightly behind her head for it simply was not efficient to have it flowing around her shoulders while she cooked and cleaned. But she did not forget she had beautiful hair. She stroked it each night with slow, thorough, long movements that kept the hair thick and lustrous. Her father had had the same beautiful thick, wavy, black hair and the same fair complexion Percy had. She remembered standing beside him as a little girl, looking into a mirror and giggling at the resemblance. She had taken such pleasure in it in those days.

But that's as far as it goes, she told herself now. *I got your hair, Papa, but I don't have to have any of the rest of you. And I don't want any of the rest of you.*

Without getting up, she tossed her brush into the open trunk. The giggling little girl in the mirror was someone else—at least it felt that way sometimes—and those memories belonged to another lifetime. Percy Morgan no longer had the luxury of indulging in sentimental moments. Giggles were not only childish but irrelevant to real life, at least to the adult life into which she had grown.

It was late. Dawn would come soon and it was imperative that she sleep. But still she feared that she would not.

eight

One morning a week later, the men burst through the mess hall door in a pack, as they had done every morning. Percy was ready for them; her days had fallen into a routine that improved steadily. The breakfast rush, which came so early in the morning, took her less by surprise every time. Exhaustion still enveloped her each night, but its onset came later and later. She might soon wish that she had something pleasurable to read in the evenings. She could reread her favorite novels, of course, or her book of poetry, the three volumes that sat on her nightstand. Her grandmother's Bible was still safely tucked away in the trunk. Grandmother would never let a day pass without reading it, but Percy had long ago given up the habit of looking for encouragement in its pages. Percy had always thought her grandmother's habit a sweet one, but after what had happened in her family, she was not sure God was someone from whom she cared to hear. Perhaps Lacey would have a book to loan her.

Percy had worked sixteen days in a row and for the first time would have an afternoon and evening off. She and Travis had agreed that twice a month she could prepare a cold supper during the day and the men would look after themselves for the evening meal. Travis even promised to assign a cleanup crew so she would find no surprises when she returned late in the evening.

The question was, though, what would she do with an entire afternoon and evening off? There were no restaurants to eat in, no concerts to attend, no parks to stroll through; and it would hardly be restful to hole up in her dingy room and pretend not to hear the commotion in the dining hall. Percy supposed she could lace up her sturdiest boots and go for a hike to explore the countryside around the camp. She had seen very little of it so far because getting the mess hall and kitchen into some semblance of order had demanded her full concentration. During the last few evenings, she had begun to imagine ways to make her small bedroom more comfortable and appealing. But she had not yet wandered off the dirt road that ran through the camp.

While she served one plate after another with sausage, biscuits, and gravy, Percy's mind planned out the details of the rest of her day. The noise and commotion that she had found deafening on her first morning barely got her attention today. She nodded somberly at the men who greeted her, averted her eyes from the ones most likely to make lewd remarks, and worked rapidly. The sooner they had their breakfast, she told herself, the sooner they would be ready to go. In the corner by the door stood the crates packed with their lunch—bread, cheese, ham, cookies, jugs of tea. She wanted to add apples to the daily lunch menu as soon as Travis could arrange to get some. Percy supposed a farmer farther south on the peninsula might be able to supply them. Apples were not something that would require sending an order to a big city.

Having inhaled their morning nourishment, the men swarmed out just the way they had swarmed in twenty minutes earlier. The mess hall was empty and quiet except for the sound of Percy clearing tables, loading dishes onto a cart, and pushing it to the kitchen. With an exasperated sigh, she realized she had forgotten to put on the big pots of water to heat so she would have hot water for cleaning up. Now her day's schedule would be delayed by at least half an hour. Percy pumped water into smaller pots, dumped them into the larger pots until they were full, stirred up the embers in the stove, and shoved in three more pieces of wood.

On an impulse, and perhaps because she was feeling agitated about the irregularity of the day, she decided to take a walk while the water heated. The mess hall was situated toward one end of the short street that ran through the camp.

She would walk briskly up one side of the street and back down the other, and as she went she would look for trails or paths that she might want to follow later. Resolutely, she wiped her hands on a dish towel, removed her apron, straightened her blue cotton skirt, and headed for the door.

The day outside was golden, the energy of spring still in the air but the strength of the morning sun bringing a promise of summer. The trees had filled out nicely with their leaves and blossoms, sending sprays of color across the road. The last wagon of lumberjacks had just rumbled out, and the dust had not quite settled in the street. Percy observed that a light sprinkling would help to tamp down the dirt without turning it to mud, the way many spring thunderstorms did.

She headed up the street. By now she knew what all the buildings were: three nice houses where real families lived; two lean-to structures where young brides waited patiently for their husbands to have time and money to build homes; the offices of Travis Gates, Peter Regals, Tom Saget, and a few others who helped to manage the business activities of the camp. Behind the mess hall were the bunkhouses where most of the men slept and at the far end, the stables and barn. Various other outbuildings dotted the landscape, and Percy knew there were more temporary shelters spread around the lumbering area.

She marched up one side of the street, making a mental note that one day she would visit Travis Gates in his office. In that professional setting, she would tell him what she needed and her plans for improving the diet of the men over the next year or so. No doubt he would be surprised to hear her talking in terms of next year; she was almost surprised herself. But she was determined to make this job work, despite the odds against it. And to do that, she had to think about the future in a way that sounded real.

Percy reached the stables, crossed the street, and started back down the other direction. Halfway back to the mess hall, she heard her name and looked up. Lacey Gates stood a few feet beyond her with a small boy in her arms.

"Good morning!" Lacey called.

"Good morning," Percy answered.

"I'm glad to see you out. I'm sure you've been busy getting settled in, but I was hoping we would have a chance to get better acquainted."

"Thank you for your unexpected hospitality on my arrival," Percy said sincerely.

"My porch is your porch," Lacey answered lightly, "any time you get hit on the head. How is your head?"

Percy touched her fingers to the spot that had been bleeding. "I'm quite recovered. It wasn't really so bad after the bleeding stopped."

"I'll be sure to tell Josh. He's been wondering."

"Oh, has he?"

"Yes. But he seemed hesitant to make a pest of himself."

"I was grateful for his help," Percy said, knowing that she had not acted very grateful on the day of her arrival or the time that Josh had come to check on her.

"This is my son, Caleb," Lacey said, turning the toddler on her hip to face Percy. "He's three."

"And you have an older one?"

"Adam. He's six. He's at my friend Abby's house."

"Abby. So that's her name. I've seen you weeding your garden together."

Lacey nodded. "I'm afraid we may have planted a bigger plot this year than we can handle. But the children are getting old enough to learn a bit about gardening. We'll soon put Nathan and Adam to work."

"It's nice that the kids have each other to play with," Percy remarked.

"Yes," Lacey agreed quickly, "and it's nice that they live so near each other. Abby and I had to go through a lot more trouble to see each other when we were small."

Percy perked up. "How long have you known Abby?"

"Nearly twenty years," Lacey answered, "since we were about nine."

"I had no idea anyone had been living in this camp so long."

Lacey laughed. "It wasn't this way twenty years ago. When Abby's father and mother moved here and brought her along, everyone thought it was scandalous. But I was delighted. I lived over at the lighthouse, several miles away. I had four brothers and no sisters. Abby and I were bosom friends as soon as we laid eyes on each other."

"And now you both live here, as neighbors."

Lacey laughed again. "When we were thirteen, we promised each other we would never marry lumberjacks. We were going to follow our dreams to the big city. But here we are—and very happy."

"It's ironic," Percy said. "I grew up in a city with thousands of people around me, and I can't think of anyone that I've known for twenty years."

"No one?"

"No, not anyone."

"Surely you must have some family, perhaps cousins or other relatives?"

Percy shook her head.

"I have cousins scattered around the state," Lacey went on. "Some of them came to visit us in the lighthouse, but that hardly ever happened. It was too hard to get to us in those days. If anyone came, they had to stay for weeks or months. We visited my grandmother in Milwaukee a few times when I was a child. I suppose I have other relatives that I don't even know about. You probably do, too." Lacey looked at Percy expectantly.

Percy shrugged. Why was Lacey so interested in her family tree? She did not offer any further information.

"I'm glad I caught you out and about," Lacey said brightly. "Travis tells me you have the evening off."

"Yes, that's right."

"Do you have plans?" Lacey said, grinning.

Percy could not help but laugh. "Well, it will be difficult to choose among the many entertaining options available to me. I thought I might take a hike and carry a picnic supper."

"Let me make you an offer you can't refuse."

"What would that be?"

"Come to our house for supper. You've already seen the back porch. Now you can see the rest of the house."

Percy's mind formed the words to decline the invitation, but before she could get them out, her heart overwhelmed her. She was lonelier than she wanted to admit. "I would love to do that," she said. "What can I bring?"

"You cook for fifty men twice a day and pack a lunch for them to take to the work site. I don't think you need to worry about bringing anything to our table."

"Perhaps one day I'll be able to return the favor," Percy said. "In the meantime, it would be delightful just to sit down to a nice meal without having to multiply a recipe times ten."

"We'll see you about six o'clock. That will give you time for a late afternoon hike, if you still want one."

"Thank you. I think I will try to do a bit of exploring."

"Stay to the trails, and you won't get lost. Most of them lead to places where the lumber has been cleared."

"I'll be sure to be careful."

Caleb's patience wore out and he squirmed to be put down. "Let's go, Mama," he said.

"Okay, Caleb. We'll go. Say good-bye to Miss Morgan."

"Good-bye, Miss Morgan," Caleb said obediently, already pumping his little legs to move down the street.

Percy waved good-bye and stood still for a moment. She was caught off guard by what had just transpired. She had not realized how anxious she was to know some of the other people in the camp, but like a neglected orphan, she found herself warming to Lacey's overtures of friendship. If there were others like Lacey, the camp would not be such a difficult place to live, after all.

nine

Percy wished for a mirror. Surely no one would think her vain for wanting to be sure her buttons were straight and her hair in place. But she had no mirror in her small room and she would have to do the best she could to dress for dinner at the Gates house. Percy had not seen an image of herself for several weeks, but from the way her sky blue dress fit her around the waist, she could tell she had lost weight. Hoping that her face did not look too thin, she pinched her cheeks for color.

The invitation to dinner had brought more nervousness than Percy thought reasonable. Why was her stomach so unsettled? Perhaps it was because she wondered if Joshua Wells would also be at dinner. Lacey had not said anything about Josh when she issued the invitation, but Percy knew he lived there and supposed he took his meals there much of the time.

She wore her hair flowing freely around her shoulders. She hardly ever let it hang loose; it was too much in the way of her work. And in the city, where she had grown up, a young woman of twenty-one would be thought childish if she let her hair hang free. But Percy was not in a city and she was in a lumber camp. Her intuition told her that city expectations would not necessarily carry over to this setting. She knew that her jet black hair was her most striking feature, and she wanted to feel pretty tonight. She stroked through her hair one last time, smoothed her skirt, and was ready to leave.

Down the street a few minutes later, she slowly ascended the steps of Lacey's front porch. It was swept clean, with two bowls of pink petunias brightening the corners. Percy felt welcome, but the swarm of butterflies in her stomach doubled. She raised her hand to knock, but the front door swung open before she could.

"You're the lady from the street," announced a child whom Percy presumed to be Adam. She had already met Caleb, and this boy was clearly older.

"And you're the boy with the sore throat," Percy retorted playfully.

Adam scowled. "It's not sore anymore."

"And I'm not in the street anymore," Percy said. "Your mother invited me to dinner."

"We're having mashed potatoes."

"Delicious. Mashed potatoes and. . .?"

"What do you mean?"

"Mashed potatoes and what else? No one eats just mashed potatoes."

"I do."

Lacey appeared behind her son. "Adam, let's invite Miss Morgan inside."

Adam hesitated a moment, glanced at his mother, and complied. "Please come in, Miss Morgan." He shuffled to one side and turned to walk away.

"We're working on manners," Lacey said softly as she gestured that Percy should enter.

Percy chuckled. "How about coming around the mess hall one evening with your lessons in manners?"

Lacey smiled. "I want to make sure Adam learns his before he gets any ideas about becoming a lumberjack."

"You don't like lumberjacks?"

"I married one," Lacey answered. "It's not the occupation so much as the setting. Standards do seem to get lax way up here. I was rather hoping that the presence of a pretty, unattached young woman would influence some of the men to be more mindful."

They walked through the house toward the kitchen.

"I suppose some of them have," Percy said. "One or two of them are trying to muster the courage to speak a flattering word to me. I see it in their eyes."

Lacey laughed aloud.

"Can I help you in the kitchen?" Percy asked. "I'm very good at mashing potatoes."

"Yes, but you do it for fifty people. There will only be six of us tonight."

Six, thought Percy. Lacey, Travis, their two sons, and herself would make five. So Josh would be there, after all.

"Besides," Lacey continued, "I invited you here to give you a break from the kitchen. The food is almost ready. I'm just waiting for Travis and Josh to come through the door."

As if on cue, the front door opened again, and the two men entered. Joshua set his black medical bag on the floor next to the door in a way that seemed habitual. "Miss Morgan, what a delightful surprise," he said. His eyes caught hers with sincerity.

"Your sister invited me to dinner when we met in the street this morning," Percy answered. She liked his eyes. An ordinary shade of brown, they nevertheless had a shining quality that caught her by surprise each time she saw them.

"I'm so glad she did."

"Travis," Lacey said, "if you can help the boys wash up, we'll be ready to eat."

"On my way," Travis said, and headed for the stairs.

"Why don't you two go on into the dining room," Lacey said. "I'll just see to the food."

Josh put his hand lightly on Percy's elbow and steered her toward the dining room.

"I see you had your medical bag with you," Percy said. "Was there an emergency today?"

Josh shook his head as he pulled out Percy's chair. He had learned his city habits well. She seated herself as gracefully as she could.

"No emergency. I make rounds a couple of times a month in some of the other places on the peninsula where people are beginning to settle. I was gone overnight, actually. It's a rather long circuit to cover in one day."

"Then you must be exhausted."

"I'm ready for a good hot meal, that's certain." Josh took his place beside Percy as Travis and the boys made their noisy entrance. Travis settled them smoothly, and the boys sat with their hands in their laps waiting for food. Lacey came in with a platter of sliced ham and the potatoes, and a promise to return with the peas and biscuits.

The boys sat across from Percy and Josh, and Lacey and Travis sat at the ends of the table. Suddenly, Percy was caught with her eyes open as everyone else closed theirs and lowered their heads. Awkwardly, she did the same.

"Father God," Travis said smoothly, "we're grateful for the gifts that You bring us every day, and tonight we're especially grateful for the gift of having Miss Morgan with us. Thank You for bringing her to our community, and bless the time that we have visiting with her tonight. Amen."

Percy felt the blush rising in her cheeks. No one had ever thanked God for her presence before.

"You like that word 'community,' don't you?" Josh said to Travis as he passed the mashed potatoes to Percy.

"Don't you?" Travis retorted.

"It's a fine word," Josh agreed, "especially for a place like this."

"What do you mean?" Percy asked. "A place like this?"

"Every year we look less and less like a lumber camp, but we're not really a town. 'Community' is a good in-between word."

Percy served herself some peas and shrugged. "I hear the men in the mess hall talking about this sometimes. But I don't see what all the fuss is about."

Josh raised an eyebrow.

"What I mean is," Percy continued, "if the camp. . .the community. . .is meant to become a town, it will. There won't be any way to stop it."

"So you believe in God's will, one way or the other?" asked Travis.

"I don't know very much about God's will," Percy was

quick to say. "I don't know very much about God at all. I just believe that some things are out of our control. No matter how much we try to control a situation, things happen. There's no stopping it."

Lacey put a spoonful of peas on Caleb's plate, despite his protest. Then she turned to Percy. "Let me ask you another question. Do you think that you can make something happen if you want to badly enough?"

Percy was quiet. "No, I don't think so," she finally said softly. "What happens, happens."

"Can God make something happen?" Josh asked.

Percy shrugged. "I don't know. I suppose He could if He cares. But God is. . .I don't know if God cares." She regretted the words as soon as she spoke them.

"I want more mashed potatoes, please," Adam said as politely as he could manage. "Please pass them to me. I can serve myself."

Travis set the bowl in front of Adam, who plopped an enormous mound of potatoes on his plate. Then he added a tiny bit more. . .and just a little more.

"There. That's enough," he announced.

Everyone laughed.

Percy was glad for the change in subject. She had not meant to express her doubts about God aloud in a roomful of strangers.

"How are you liking your work, Miss Morgan?" Josh asked.

"I'm slowly getting squared away," she answered, relieved that he did not pursue her earlier remarks.

"The men are raving about your cooking," Travis reported, "behind your back, of course."

"Of course," Percy echoed, smiling. "To tell me to my face would be almost like being glad I came."

"You have a good attitude. I appreciate that."

"I have a lot of ideas for how we could give the men a better diet," Percy said. "I would like to plant a vegetable garden, but it would have to be rather large to feed fifty men. We could plant herbs, too, so everything would not taste so bland. And if I had a second pair of hands in the kitchen at meal-time, I could offer more variety."

"Didn't the cook used to have an assistant?" Lacey asked.

Travis nodded. "No one seems to want the job right now."

"Those silly men don't want to be told what to do by a woman," Lacey said irritably.

Travis's eyes twinkled. "They'll never manage marriage if they don't get over that."

"What about one of the new brides?" Josh suggested. "Maybe both of them."

Lacey shook her head. "What they need is friendship, not more work. Keeping house in those lean-tos is no picnic, and they both hope to begin building soon."

"Well, perhaps I'll ask around among the men again," Travis said. "Percy should have help."

"That was easier than I thought," Percy said pleasantly.

"Getting Travis to agree with you is not the hard part," Josh reminded her. "We still have to find someone who would like the job."

"Until we do, I'll press on by myself. I'm going to mark off a garden plot tomorrow."

Percy looked across at Adam and burst out laughing. He had energetically attacked his mound of potatoes and had eaten a good portion of it. But a V-shaped clump hung from his chin like a white beard. "Perhaps when this community becomes a town, you'll find a good barber for your son."

ten

Not a scoop of mashed potatoes remained in the bowl, and the bread basket was empty, but there were some peas left. Everyone had eaten their fill and the boys had wandered into the living room to play.

"This is a beautiful home," Percy remarked to her hostess. "And you've decorated it wonderfully. You have a flair for the artistic."

"Thank you," Lacey said, "but most of the credit belongs to my husband and my friend Abby's husband. They built it and they wouldn't settle for anything less than the best in craftsmanship."

"I can see that they are skilled. We had a carved crown molding like this in the house I grew up in, and my father always told people it had come from Europe."

"Ah, your secret is out," Travis said, smiling. "You're a civilized city girl, after all. Do you miss all the finery?"

"I'm quite content to be here," Percy said sincerely, without further explanation about what had brought her to the camp.

"Do your parents still live in that home?" Lacey asked.

Percy hesitated a split second. "No," she finally said, "they've moved on." She lifted her eyes to the large dining room windows dressed with a rich burgundy tapestry. "Did you make these draperies yourself?"

"Yes, she did," Travis answered proudly for his wife. "My mother-in-law, before she passed away, made sure Lacey could do just about anything."

"She just thought of it as doing what was necessary," Lacey said.

Percy was relieved that her question about the draperies had successfully shifted the focus of conversation. What had possessed her to bring up her childhood home in the first place? Danger lurked in places where she began to feel comfortable. She would have to be more careful.

"What else did she teach you?" Percy asked, trying to make sure the conversation did not circle back to her family.

"Cooking, gardening, wood chopping. She did it all."

"Did she grow up on a farm?"

"No, actually she was a city girl, too, like you. My father wooed her up here to the end of the world. Thirty years ago, there was very little this far north except the lighthouse. We had to be even more self-sufficient than we are now."

"Who taught her how to get along so well?"

"Experience," Lacey answered quickly. "Especially after she started having children, she had to learn very quickly."

"Don't forget that your mother is also the one who made a teacher out of you," Travis said. He turned to Percy. "Mary Wells taught all five of her children, and they are five of the most well-rounded people I know."

"I think Lacey deserves the credit for Micah's education," Joshua said. "She helped a lot when Micah was small and then picked up where Mama had left off when she died. But Mama probably would have insisted on teaching me a medical course if she had not become ill and died before I was ready for medical school."

Percy turned to Josh and smiled. "She sounds like a wonderful mother." Images of her own mother floated through her mind, a mother who knew very little about what the private tutors might be teaching her daughters and who was as isolated from realities of the world as if she had lived in a lighthouse.

"Mama was very strict," Josh was saying. "We did not always appreciate that as we were growing up, but I can see now that it gave us the determination that we needed to do what we're doing now."

"And what exactly are you doing now?" Percy teased.

"Building a town," Josh declared emphatically.

"Or at the very least a community," Travis added. "Right now, I would like a community with a softer chair." He pushed back from the table.

"Go on into the living room," Lacey said, as she stood and began stacking plates. "Get comfortable, and I'll bring coffee."

"I'll help you," Percy offered. She picked up the empty mashed potatoes bowl. "I guess we don't have to worry much about the leftovers."

Lacey laughed. "Adam's favorite food. He won't be pleased when he finds out that there are enough peas left to have them again tomorrow."

"Are these from your garden?" Percy asked as they walked with their loads toward the kitchen.

"I canned them last year," Lacey explained. "I can't wait for this year's crop to be ready. There's nothing like sugar snap peas, fresh from the pod."

"Perhaps you'll help me plant my garden," Percy said hopefully. "I've never actually had a vegetable garden before."

Lacey burst out laughing. She set her armful of plates beside the sink. "You sounded like such an expert when you asked Travis about putting in a garden."

Percy shook her head. "No expert, just being sensible. I have to have more than an occasional ear of corn if I'm going to cook properly, and a vegetable and herb garden seems like the most economical way to improve the diet for the men in the long run."

"You're right about that. We can get a lot of food in cans now, but fresh is always so nice. Travis should be impressed that you are thinking ahead and trying to keep costs down at the same time."

"So you'll help me?"

"Yes, I'll be delighted to help, and I'll tell Abby that she's got to help, too."

"Can you mark it off with me in the morning?"

"Certainly."

"Good. Then I just need to find someone willing to work

with me to look after it."

Lacey took the serving dishes from Percy's hand. "Go on into the living room."

"But I'll be happy to help you clean up," Percy said.

"No thanks. Not now, at least. I'll make coffee and join you in a few minutes."

Percy could see that Lacey was not one to be argued with. She turned to go into the living room. She stood under the hand-carved crown molding and soaked up the scene before her eyes.

Travis sat in a chair that was obviously his favorite, his feet up on an ottoman, with a book in his lap. But he was not reading it. He was watching Joshua and the boys. Josh sat cross-legged on one side of a checkerboard, while Adam squirmed around on the other side.

"You've got me now," Josh said dramatically. "I don't know how I'll ever get myself out of this predicament."

Adam howled with pleasure.

"My turn, my turn," Caleb insisted.

"You're not playing," Adam said emphatically.

"Of course he is," Josh said, grabbing Caleb and pulling him into his lap. "If I ever needed someone on my team, it's now."

Caleb gave his brother a smug, satisfied look.

"What shall we do, Caleb?" Josh asked. "Should we move this one or that one?"

The three-year-old boy put a pudgy finger on a red checker. "This one."

"This one? Are you sure?"

Caleb nodded.

"All right, we'll move this one." Josh slid the checker diagonally one space.

Adam whooped and he swept down his hands to double jump his uncle and come in for a king.

Caleb turned around and patted his uncle's head. "It's okay, Uncle Josh. Next time."

"That's right. We'll get him next time."

The lump in Percy's throat was so big she could barely swallow. What a wonderful picture of a man with his children—only these were not Joshua's sons, but his nephews. She could not imagine he could be any better with them if they were his own. Travis looked on with a smile, much more interested in his sons than his book.

The house she had grown up in may have had hand-carved European crown moldings and expensive arrangements of fine furniture, but it did not have what she saw before her eyes right now. She herself had learned to play checkers by reading a book and deciphering the rules and illustrations on her own. She had practiced against herself until she could predict all possibilities. But her father would never have come home from the bank and then spend his evening playing checkers with young children, much less seek obviously futile advice from a three-year-old boy. He rarely even stayed in the same room with his daughters after the somber, formal evening meal, preferring instead to withdraw to his study until long after Percy and her sister had been sent upstairs to bed. Percy had learned at a very young age not to disturb her father when he went into his study. But that was then, and this was now. What did it matter, anyway? she asked herself.

"Can we play again?" Adam asked. He looked at his uncle with the same hopeful brown eyes that Josh had.

"Sure, we can play again," Josh answered. "This time, Caleb gets to make the first move. Maybe we'll be luckier."

They started setting up the game and Percy took a step forward. "Who taught you how to play checkers?" she asked Josh teasingly.

"My father," he answered. "But it looks like I could use a few more lessons."

Adam did not want to stop playing, so he set up one game after another. Percy could not help but be drawn into the competition and, by the time they were finished with dessert and coffee, Percy was sitting in for Josh, having proved herself to be a worthy opponent for Adam.

As Percy played, though, she kept one ear cocked to the adult conversation. Travis was mulling over whom he might ask to work in the kitchen with Percy. Josh was pressing to move forward with some new construction, following Peter's latest drawings. So far the people responsible for the lumbering business were responsible for the growing community, Josh remarked. But soon the community would need its own mayor. The people who lived in the town should have some say in how it developed.

Percy had no plans to leave any time soon, but, at the same time, she had not thought about the future of the camp. She wondered if she would ever be personally interested in how it developed.

The time came when Percy faced Josh over the checkerboard, with everyone else cheering over their competition. With most of the pieces removed from the board, she knew she had him cornered before any one figured out the strategy. She could make a subtle move and lose the game graciously in another three or four moves or she could easily win it within three moves. As she contemplated her choice, Percy glanced at Josh's gentle face and comfortable smile. He was a good, kind man who deserved to win. But she had earned this win; she had not practiced by herself all those years for nothing! So she made the move that would bring her victory, but Josh did not immediately realize the impending defeat. When it came, though, he groaned but accepted it graciously, catching her eye with the twinkle in his.

Percy lingered in the warmth of the Gates home as long as she dared without being impolite. The butterflies in her stomach had long ago disappeared. Even as she moved her feet down the porch steps and across the street, she felt the reluctance of her body to leave the congenial, welcome atmosphere of that simple living room. At the back of the mess hall, she sighed and then opened the narrow door to her little room. She thought of Lacey's rich burgundy draperies. Perhaps after the garden was in, she would ask Lacey to teach her to sew. If she could learn to cook as well as she did out of necessity, she might also conquer sewing.

She removed her dress, hung it on a peg, and pulled her simple cotton nightdress over her head. For so many years, she had not allowed herself the luxury of an evening like this one. It was not a fancy evening—they had eaten simple food and played simple games—but it was the best evening Percy Morgan had had for years. She had felt welcome—and she had almost forgotten how good that could feel.

eleven

The promise of a real summer infused the air. As Percy bent over the washtub behind the mess hall, scrubbing her kitchen towels and rags and the aprons that protected her few dresses, sweat trickled down her temples. In an attempt to keep the sweat from dripping down her neck, she scrunched up one side of her face, but without her hands free, there was little she could do to control the rivulets of perspiration. Even before plunging her hands into the scalding wash water, the close, humid air had Percy feeling like a shriveled human blister, and it had curled her hair in sticky knots around her face. She imagined that with a proper brushing, the hair framing her face could be arranged in a very flattering way on a day like this. But she had no time for brushing and she still had no mirror in her room. She certainly did not feel very attractive, hunched over a wash basin with her hair roughly knotted at the back of her neck to keep it out of her way, her sleeves shoved up past her elbows, and her blouse unbuttoned at the neck to catch the rare hint of a breeze.

Percy had not expected such miserable weather for late spring; actually, she was not prepared for it at all. Lacey told her that this was just the beginning of a brutal summer. Lacey's description of the extreme summer weather had seemed exaggerated to Percy and she had been determined not to be frightened off by it. Surely the proximity to water would have some cooling effect. Where Percy came from, being near the ocean made all the difference. But Lacey was proving to be right; Percy should never have doubted the word of someone who had spent twenty-eight years living here. She longed for a walk along the water, closer to the areas where the men were out logging. Perhaps then she could hope for a flutter of a breeze. Between the hot kitchen and the labor of laundry, Percy found little relief from the heat and humidity. She could only imagine what it must be like for the men, laboring unsheltered in the hot sun for long hours each day. Each night they returned to the mess hall, wilted and somber, until refreshed by nourishment and cold drinks.

If this was only the beginning, Percy hated to think what the rest of the summer might be like. It certainly would not remind her of the summers of her childhood. There would be no leisurely games of croquet on the front lawn. Actually, no one in the lumber camp had a front lawn, least of all the mess hall where Percy's cramped quarters were squeezed. There would be no tall glasses of lemonade carried out to her by the family cook, no fanciful games with her little sister under the shade of a spreading oak tree, no books to tickle her imagination. This summer would be work, all work, and Percy could not allow herself to imagine anything different.

True to her word, Lacey helped Percy mark off a vegetable garden the day after their dinner together. While Lacey and Abby had put in their garden weeks ago, Lacey was quite optimistic that it was not too late for Percy to grow a few things, if she was careful what she planted. The garden plot was not large. Percy had wanted a plot four times as large and Lacey had laughed aloud and told Percy that she was not talking about a garden but a farm. Percy had argued that she needed a large plot in order to raise enough vegetables for all the men, but Lacey insisted that what Percy had in mind would be far more work than one person could handle, even if that person was the stubborn Percy Morgan. Reluctantly, Percy yielded to Lacey's advice. She had cornered off one section for growing herbs; even if she could not produce enough vegetables to feed fifty men all winter, she could at least flavor the food she prepared with more variety.

As much as Percy hated to admit it, Lacey's caution made sense. This was her first garden, after all, and perhaps there was more to the task than simply planting, watering, and enjoying the sun. At the moment, she did not find the sun very enjoyable and would have preferred to water herself rather than vegetables. Once the garden was planted, she would be obligated to weed it, also. Already Percy was planning how she might alter her routine in order to work the garden in the cooler evening.

In the past, she had not thought too much about gardens. Her own mother had spent many summer days on a lounge chair in the middle of a flower garden, but as Percy reflected on the memory, she realized she had never seen her mother actually work in the garden. A quiet, unobtrusive older man came in periodically to tend to the garden. He produced beautiful, exotic flowers that Percy's mother proudly displayed as if they were the work of her own hands. As she was growing up, it had never occurred to Percy to wonder where her vegetables came from, and she was never curious where the cook had gotten them from in the first place. In fact, she spent much of her childhood wishing her vegetables would go away.

Percy's mother had not done a lot of the things that Percy now did every day. It was a good thing that she had occasionally watched when the wash was done, Percy reflected, for she had turned out not to be completely helpless. Her observation skills and quick intelligence put her in good stead when she had to learn something new rapidly and furtively.

Percy squinted at the sun and realized immediately that she had to return to the stifling kitchen because the men would be appearing for their evening meal any moment. She abandoned the wash, thinking that she might return to it later in the evening when it might be cooler anyway.

Inside the mess hall, Percy barely got the food off the stove and onto the large serving platters before the men came tumbling in. After a quiet day with her own thoughts, their noise jolted her. Today they entered with even more rambunctiousness than usual, and Percy immediately realized that it was not friendly camaraderie. The voices were pitched loud and boisterous. Her eyes wide and alert, she pushed through the swinging doors that led from the kitchen to the main dining room. The food line had begun to form, and Percy could see immediately that the men in line were those who preferred quiet and solitude at the end of the day. They were not likely to be involved in the argument growing rapidly behind them.

Quickly, Percy began to serve food. Knowing that she had plenty, she heaped large servings on the plates. Normally she simply set out a stack of plates and let the men serve themselves. Today she tried to create a diversion of her own, keeping one eye on the men huddled by the door who seemed not to be interested in eating. Troy Wilger's face was as red as she had ever seen it, and Carson Gregory had his nose right up against Troy's.

"I'm afraid I'm not used to the heat and humidity you have here," Percy said loudly and with contrived cheerfulness. "I can't imagine how you men have the stamina to work in the heat all day long."

Two men quietly took their plates and headed for a table in the corner. No one responded to Percy's attempt at conversation.

"It will be quite a challenge for me," she continued, even more loudly, "to come up with some meals that will refresh you when you come in for supper."

The shuffling by the door swelled alarmingly. Men lined up behind Troy and Carson.

"What's going on?" Percy finally asked quietly as Matt Harden came through the line. "What are they so upset about?"

Matt scowled. "It's this town business. Peter Regals was out at the site today talking the way he always does."

"What do you mean?" Percy had barely met Abby's husband, but he had not struck her as someone who would incite a crowd. Josh and Lacey seemed to like Peter's ideas.

"He had some crazy ideas about a town government," Matt explained reluctantly. "Something about how everyone should have a say in how things are done around here."

"Isn't that good?" Percy asked. She gave Matt an extra scoop of mashed potatoes.

Matt shrugged. "Peter says the family that owns the lumber company is not trying to own us body and soul. A real town up here would be good for all of us, but some of the others, well, they're not convinced."

"No?"

He shook his head. "They figure Peter and his father-in-law and Travis Gates will run things the way they want them, no matter what the rest of us think."

The smack of a fist against a jaw interrupted their conversation. Carson Gregory stumbled and fell back against a row of chairs, scattering them with a clatter. Immediately, he scrambled to his feet and charged at Troy Wilger. With his head bent low, Carson slammed into Troy's midsection, but the hefty tall man barely moved under the impact of the smaller, lighter man. Instead, the two of them entwined their arms and pushed and twisted their way across the room. In only a few seconds they had broken through the food line and began circling the food table. Their tussle showed no sign of letting up; determination burned in both their faces.

"Stop that right now!" Percy demanded, but they ignored her.

The men in line, not wanting to heighten the hostility, stepped back. The entourage surrounding Troy and Carson followed the struggling pair across the room and crowded around the table. Percy was forced to leap out of the way herself.

Troy got the upper hand and planted his massive hands firmly on Carson's shoulders. With one great shove, Troy threw Carson through the air. Carson came down with a crash on the serving table, which gave way and split down the middle. Percy's serving dishes clattered to the floor, spilling chicken and potatoes. The pies she had labored over all afternoon splattered the floor and were flattened as Carson landed on top of them.

Ignoring his bleeding lip and the apples and potatoes stuck to his backside, Carson scrambled to his feet once again and lurched at Troy. Troy deftly stepped out of the way, and the angry Carson plunged into another row of chairs. The men watching began to cheer. Carson came up swinging. Clearly, there was no way he could win a fight against Troy Wilger, but Percy could see the fire in his eyes and he was not about to give up. Around her, men laughed and cheered, oblivious to the fact that their own meals had been lost to a fight that most of them cared little about.

Percy whirled around, dashed into the kitchen, and returned with her heaviest iron pot and spoon. Fiercely she banged the pot like a drum. Some of the men began to chuckle at her, but she ignored them. Using the pot as a shield, she ventured toward Troy and Carson. One way or another, she was going to stop this fight.

Her opening came and she took it. She aimed low. With all her might, she slammed her heavy metal spoon into Troy Wilger's kneecap. He stopped and stared at her. Knowing that he was more likely startled than actually hurt, she wasted no time making her point.

"I don't care whether this is a town or not," she shouted. "I do know that it is not a zoo, and I will not have you acting like wild animals in the middle of my dining room."

Percy glared first at Troy, then at Carson. "I made one supper tonight and I don't intend to make another one. The two of you can explain to your buddies why they have to go to bed hungry tonight. As for me, I'm finished for the day!" She threw down her pot and let it clatter and roll across the floor; it echoed rancorously around the room. "I'm going out. When I come back, I expect that this mess the two of you have created will be cleaned up. I'd better not find a sliver of apple on this floor or a splinter of wood from the table you ruined. Clean it up! I mean it!"

She spun around and marched out the front door, feeling the stares that followed her on the back of her hot neck but refusing to acknowledge them.

Outside the door, she was just ready to let her shoulders sag with the weight and frustration she really felt when she spotted Josh Wells coming around the corner.

"What's going on?" he asked. "What's all the commotion?"

Percy kept her shoulders rigid and her head high. Without breaking stride, she replied, "Nothing I can't handle."

twelve

Percy stayed away for long, exhausting hours; she certainly was in no hurry to return to the mess hall and face the remains of the chaos to which she may have contributed. The evening was warm and sticky, so she had no need for shelter. From her perch on a boulder tucked at the edge of the woods, she could see the dim lights of Lacey and Travis's home. Percy knew she would be welcome there, but somehow the thought of being with other people exhausted her. Besides, she did not want Travis to charge over and let the men believe she had tattled on them. No doubt Josh had gone into the dining hall to see why she had flown out the way she did. Travis and Lacey would hear about the fiasco soon enough. Instead, she sat alone, her arms around her knees, and stared up at the night sky.

What was out there? she wondered. Were the planets real? Could they really be hanging in the black space that overwhelmed her? Was God real? Was He out there somewhere? Mrs. Higgins, her Sunday school teacher for most of her childhood, had assured Percy and the rest of the class that God was indeed out there. But Percy was not so sure. If He was, then why had her life taken the turns it had? Why had she ended up breaking up fistfights in an obscure place instead of entertaining suitors in a more genteel setting?

Eventually Percy trudged back up to the mess hall. In her haste to leave, she had not thought to take a lantern with her, and she was guided only by the stars she found so mysterious. With a grimace on her face and reluctance in her hands, she pulled the door open and entered. Blackness greeted her, just as deep as the blackness outside. She crept along the side wall to a window ledge where she knew she would find a candle to light. By its dim flame, she peered around the large room. The tables were upright with chairs pushed in neatly. The serving table, splintered by Carson Gregory's smashing fall, had been removed. Pots, platters, and leftover food were gone from sight. The room looked as if nothing unusual had happened that night—except that one table was missing. With a sigh of disbelief and relief, Percy crept through the immaculate kitchen and went to bed.

ta

In the morning, Percy served breakfast as usual and did not speak of the previous evening. Troy Wilger and Carson Gregory clearly avoided her, coming to the newly designated serving table to pick up a plate of pancakes and staying only as briefly as necessary. Percy set a platter of fresh pancakes in front of Troy but said nothing. The other men were reserved. Few lifted their eyes to Percy's. Her glare dared anyone to approach her.

Later, as Percy worked in the garden, meticulously preparing the ground for the vegetable seeds Travis would bring, Lacey approached with a grin on her face. While no one was speaking to Percy, apparently the men were speaking to each other. Troy and Carson's behavior was extreme, but expected, according to Lacey, and they had come to blows before. But no one had expected the spitfire that Percy had shown. Lacey found it hilarious that the men had complied with her demands that they clean up after themselves. According to what Lacey had heard from Josh, who had gone into the mess hall to investigate after passing Percy, Troy and Carson had done most of the cleanup work themselves. Percy was the talk of the town, so to speak.

But Percy did not want to be the talk of the town. She simply wanted peace and order in the dining hall. So, over the next few days, she proceeded with her usual routine, including the added task of tending to the garden. The dirt oozing between her fingers was strangely comforting, and keeping her fingers busy and her eyes focused helped to stem the swirling in her mind. Her nerves needed calming, especially today. She had accepted an invitation from Lacey to spend the early afternoon at the Gates home with Lacey, Abby, and Bridget and Moriah, the two young brides living in lean-tos while their husbands prepared to build homes. Abby's mother, the first woman to come to the lumber camp more than twenty years ago, would also join them. Percy had baked a pie, which was cooling in the kitchen. Knowing that she had only a few minutes left in solitude, she breathed deeply of the earthy air and exhaled slowly.

As she let out her sigh, Percy was jolted by the raucous sound of a horse and wagon careening down the street. What she heard was no gentle trot and the rhythm of turning wheels. It was a full gallop and the clatter of a wagon being stretched beyond its capacity. The shouting voices demanded immediate attention. Her heart thumping, Percy sprang to her feet and hustled around to the front of the mess hall.

"Where's Josh?" Matt Harden demanded. "Find Josh!" He dropped the reins and hurtled himself off the wagon bench. The horse seemed agitated, but he paid no attention.

"What's happened?" Percy asked urgently. She followed Matt as he hurried around to the back and then hopped up into the wagon bed.

"An accident with the saw," Matt answered. "It went out of control. He's hurt bad."

Matt huddled over the victim and Percy strained to see who the injured man was. She saw the ashen face of Troy Wilger.

Peter Regals was in the street now, and Travis Gates was right behind him, having left the office where they both spent their days.

"We have to find Josh," Matt repeated. "He's bleedin' bad."

"I'll go look for Josh," Percy offered. "He must be at Lacey's house."

Peter shook his head. "He's gone on one of his circuits. He left this morning."

Matt flashed a look of anxiety. "There can't be anybody who needs him as much as Troy does right now."

"He's been gone a couple of hours," Peter said. "I don't know if we can catch him."

"We have to try," Matt insisted. "That old mare of his is half blind. He can't have gone all that far in two hours if he was stopping to check on folks. He said he came back to doctor us, and right now Troy needs a doctor. Which way did he go?"

"He usually heads straight south first," Peter answered. "There's a woman in a little place along the harbor who's due to have a baby any day now. My guess is that he went to check on her."

"I know the place," Matt said. He grabbed at the wagon hitch and set the horse free. "Take him somewhere," he instructed. "Make him comfortable. I'll be back with Josh."

Matt jumped on the horse and galloped off. Peter scrambled up into the wagon and put his hand under Troy's head.

"Where is the wound?" Travis asked, unwrapping the blanket from around Troy.

"It's his leg," Peter exclaimed. "It's cut deeply. Someone had the good sense to tie a tourniquet above the wound."

"His clothes are drenched," Travis said. "He's already lost a lot of blood."

"What can we do?" Percy asked.

"Matt is right. We should take him somewhere and get him comfortable?"

"Where?"

"Wherever we take him, he'll have to stay awhile," Peter said. "He's going to need a lot of care."

"I'm afraid our back porch just won't do," Travis said. "Besides, it's too far up the street. Matt took the horse. We don't have time to fetch another one to hitch the wagon to."

Travis and Peter looked at each other, then at Percy. "We'll have to take him to the mess hall," Peter said. "We're right here in front of it."

"Yes, and there's plenty of water and clean rags," Travis

said. "We can start trying to get him cleaned up so Josh can see what he's doing."

"The mess hall?" Percy echoed faintly.

"Percy," Travis said gently, "I'm afraid we're going to need your bed for a while."

"My bed?" Indignation rose within her. How dare they invade the only private space she had—and for Troy Wilger!

"I know it's an inconvenience," Travis said. "But right now, taking him there makes the most sense."

"You're right," Peter agreed. He placed his hands under Troy's shoulder. "Help me carry him. Percy, you get the door."

Numbly, she followed their instructions. She held open the door as Peter and Travis carried Troy as quickly and gently as possible, then she led the way back to her little room. They laid him on the bed.

"We need rags," Travis said, "and hot water. Do you have any on the stove?"

Percy rallied. Travis was right. The mess hall was well supplied to care for the injured man.

"Yes, of course," she said. "I'll be right back." She scurried into the kitchen and scooped up a handful of dish towels, knowing that she might never again be able to use them in the kitchen. She filled a small pot with water and returned to the bedroom as quickly as she could. "Here, start with these. The water is not hot, but I'll put some on to heat."

"Troy!" Travis called loudly. "Troy, can you hear me?"

There was no response.

"He's out cold," Peter said. "He's lost too much blood. We've got to get these clothes off of him and make sure the bleeding has stopped. Percy, bring me your kitchen shears."

Once again Percy followed instructions. Then she returned to the kitchen long enough to stoke up the stove fire and pump water into a pot. Back in the bedroom, she found Peter and Travis slicing through the sticky mess of Troy's denim pants. She grimaced and her stomach lurched as they exposed the wound. The saw had cut deeply into Troy's thigh.

"How could this happen?" she asked.

"That doesn't matter right now," Peter answered. "We just have to take care of him and pray that Joshua gets here soon."

Percy's head spun as she looked at the clock on her bedroom wall. How much time had passed since Matt took off in search of Josh? It couldn't have been more than a few minutes, but it already felt like hours. A few minutes earlier, she had been anticipating a leisurely afternoon with the few other women around her. Now a man she strongly disliked was lying on her bed, helpless and at her mercy. In a moment, her life had changed.

She closed her eyes against the thought of what this change might mean. She had not yet recovered from the last time that her life had changed in an instant.

Where was Josh?

thirteen

For more than three hours, Peter, Travis, and Percy tended Troy Wilger, whose consciousness rose and fell at random intervals and endured only briefly. When he was awake, the unbearable pain and blood loss soon drove him to the respite of unconsciousness again. While he lay limp on the bed, Peter and Travis huddled over his wounds. They had cut away his soiled dungarees and stemmed the bleeding enough to loosen the tourniquet and restore circulation to the leg. The wound gaped open, ugly and vicious. The blood flow was no longer rapid, but the fact that it still seeped concerned everyone. They changed the cloths every few minutes. Percy was running out of clean rags to offer.

Peter and Travis speculated on the facts of the accident. Had Troy been working the saw and lost control? His years of experience made that seem unlikely. Was Carson Gregory on the other end of the saw and had he deliberately become aggressive? They hated to think Carson was capable of such maliciousness. Peter and Travis shook their heads in befuddlement, realizing the pointlessness of their speculation. They would have to wait until they could gather the facts. Besides, what they needed most right now was not an explanation but a doctor.

Every few minutes Percy restlessly raised her eyes to the door frame, hoping to see Josh. Several times one of the vigil keepers went outside to look down the street, hoping to catch sight of him and signal where he should come. Finally, Josh exploded through the front door. Percy heard his thundering steps as he crashed across the wooden planks of the mess hall floor. Her heart in her throat, she met him in the kitchen.

"What happened?" he asked urgently as he pushed his way past her.

"We're not sure. We thought Matt might have told you."

He shook his head. "There was no time. He only said that it was very bad."

"It is."

By this time Josh had squeezed into her little bedroom to see for himself. Travis and Peter lurched to their feet. With Troy on the bed and four people standing, the room was crowded. Josh pushed his way past the others and knelt at the side of the bed to examine the wound.

"Matt was right," he soon announced. "It's a serious wound."

"Will he lose the leg?" Peter asked anxiously.

Josh sighed. "I hope not. I'm going to try to sew it back together. Let's pray there's been no chance for gangrene to set in." He set his medical bag solidly on the floor beside him and swiftly opened it.

"How much help will you need?" Travis asked.

"I need one of you to stay," Josh answered without looking up. "It's too warm and dark and crowded in here with all of you here. Travis, you and Peter go find out what happened. Percy can stay with me."

Percy was about to protest, but Travis cut her off. "Good. I would like to ride out and see if anyone saw what happened. If I hear anything that leads me to think this was intentional—"

"Don't jump to conclusions," Peter warned. "Accidents happen, even to someone as experienced as Troy Wilger."

Travis blew out his breath. "You're right. But I do want to get the facts straight. If it was an accident, we want to be sure it won't happen to anyone else."

"Percy, I'm going to need better light," Josh said, ignoring the interchange between Travis and Peter. "See how many lamps you can round up."

"Of course," she choked out in response. "And I'll pull back the curtains as far as they'll go to let in the daylight."

"Yes, yes." Josh was fishing in his bag for supplies. "Has he been conscious at all?"

"A few times, but only briefly."

Travis and Peter had left and it was up to Percy to report on Troy's condition and care. She lit the light at the side of her bed and scraped the table across the floor closer to Josh.

"I have two more lamps in the kitchen," Percy said. "I'll get them."

Josh nodded but did not speak. His fingers gently probed the wound. When Percy returned with the extra lamps, he said, "You did a good job cleaning up the wound."

"Peter and Travis did that," Percy quickly clarified. "I just brought them water and clean rags."

Josh's eyes went briefly to the pile of blood-soaked rags in the corner of Percy's bedroom. The bedding was streaked with blood and the mud caked on Troy's clothing. Her counted cross stitch throw pillow was tossed haphazardly on the floor in the far corner. Travis and Peter had repositioned her trunk in order to sit on it, and when Josh arrived, he had shoved it out of the way. Now it sat cockeyed across the center of the room.

"I'm sure this is not quite the décor you had in mind for this room," he said.

Percy shrugged. "It'll clean up." Hours ago, she had resigned herself to the reality of what was happening, bizarre as it was.

"You're being a good sport about this invasion of your home."

Percy laughed. "I didn't really have a choice." She was caught off guard by Josh's reference to her room as her home for she had not yet come to think of it in that way. Although she had nowhere else to go, no other place to call home, and had no plans for leaving, she had not thought of this room as "home" in her own mind. Would she ever? Would she ever know the feeling of being at home again?

"It's a good thing he's unconscious," Josh said. "This is going to hurt."

"What if he wakes up?" Percy asked, suddenly panicked.

"Let's pray he doesn't. And if he does, we'll use ether.

Look in my bag for a small pair of scissors," Josh instructed. "I'm going to start stitching. I'll need you to help cut every now and then. Get in here as close as you can so you can see what I'm doing, but don't block the light."

"But I'm not. . .I've never—"

"Percy, I need your help."

Josh's tone was clear. He was not leaving her any choice, any more than she had had a choice about any of the day's events so far. Swallowing hard, she knelt on the floor next to him, feeling his shoulder against hers.

Josh worked on the wound and Percy hardly breathed as she watched him sew the gaping hole together, layer by layer. At his instruction she snipped, cleaned, adjusted the light, wiped his brow.

Finally, they finished. Josh rocked back off his knees and sat on the floor cross-legged. He held his bloodied hands carefully out away from his body.

"Here," Percy said, thrusting a pot of water toward him. It was no longer hot, but at least Josh could rinse off. "I'll heat some more."

"Thank you," he said.

Percy put another pot of water on the stove. She returned to find Josh shaking the water off his hands and she handed him a clean towel.

"You could use some of this water yourself," he said.

For the first time, Percy looked at her own hands and clothing. The dress was a dark one and perhaps the blood stains would not show too badly after it was washed.

"I'm sorry about all this mess," Josh said.

"It's not your fault. I'm just glad you got here."

"I wish I had been here sooner. I could have made my rounds tomorrow."

"You can't possibly know when something is going to happen here. I heard you went to check on a pregnant woman."

He nodded. "She's fine, but her time is getting close."

"You did the right thing to go."

"I'm going to insist that Peter begin building the medical clinic he's been promising. He must start right away."

"Even if you had a clinic," Percy pointed out, "you would have been away."

"Perhaps. But you and Peter and Travis would have had a proper place to take Troy and the right supplies to help him until I got there. People have to know where to find help. Matt could have taken Troy straight to the clinic. And I need proper working conditions for situations like this." He gestured around. "Bright lights, a place to operate, a bed where a patient can recover and I can stay close."

A groan coming from the bed snatched their attention. Percy watched, her own eyes wide, as Troy opened his eyes and stared at her. "What's she doing here?" Troy asked gruffly.

Josh looked at Percy. "Has he spoken before?"

She shook her head. "This is the first time."

Josh turned back to Troy. "You should be thankful she's here. She's been very conscientious about taking care of you."

"I didn't ask her to."

"You were not in a position to ask anybody anything," Josh said harshly. "Just be grateful someone was around to look after you."

"That's your job," Troy muttered.

"You've been unconscious a long time," Josh said. "This is one time when you don't need an argument."

"What happened to my leg? It's throbbing with pain."

"The wound was very deep and I had to sew it back together. I'm hopeful for a full recovery."

"Where am I?" Troy grunted.

"In Miss Morgan's room, behind the mess hall," Josh informed him. "Another reason why you should be grateful to her."

"I want to get out of here."

Josh shook his head. "Oh, no. You're not going anywhere for quite a while."

Percy's heart lurched. What did Josh mean? Surely he was

not going to leave Troy Wilger in her bedroom!

Josh looked at Percy. "I'm sorry, Percy. But he's very, very weak. I can't move him for several days, maybe even a week."

She gulped. "So you want him to stay here? In my room?"

Josh nodded. "I realize it's an extreme inconvenience, and I'll do my best to make it up to you. I'm not sure where we'll take him for the recovery period he's going to need, but at least for the time being, he must stay here. I'll stay with him much of the time, of course."

"But. . .but. . . ." Percy could not put words around the cloud of feelings that swirled inside her mind. Joshua's reasons for usurping her room were quite legitimate, but to have the only private space she had taken from her seemed equally unreasonable.

"You can stay in my room at Lacey's house," Josh explained, as if reading her thoughts. "You can move in over there right now, if you want to. Plan to stay a few days. Travis can explain to Lacey, if he hasn't already. I'm sure she'll understand."

Percy hardly knew what to say.

"Why don't you get a few things together," Josh said softly, "at least enough for tonight. You can always come back for whatever you need."

Of course Josh was right, Percy told herself. What he suggested made perfect sense. She looked from Joshua to Troy, who was drifting back to sleep.

"Just take what you need," Josh repeated. "Don't worry about the mess. I promise it won't be here in the morning. Just go on over to Lacey's."

Percy gasped. "Oh, no! I was supposed to go to Lacey's hours ago. She invited me for the afternoon with the other women. I made a pie to take."

"You could still take it."

Percy glanced at the clock, suddenly mindful of time. "I barely have time to make supper for the men. They'll be here before I know it."

"I wish there were someone else who could do that for you," Josh said gently. "You must be exhausted." Josh's weary face, lined with worry about Troy Wilger, nevertheless looked at Percy with sincere concern.

Percy's knees were weak, her stomach lurching, her head pounding. Yes, she was exhausted. "I'll be fine," she said a little stiffly. "I'll check on that hot water so you can clean up properly. Then I've got to get back to work."

fourteen

Percy thought the men would never finish the biscuits and sausage gravy she had hastily thrown together for supper. Since she usually served that meal for breakfast, she got a few strange looks as men came through the line. But she had needed something that she could make without thinking, without calculating or multiplying ingredients. Finally, the last dishes were cleaned up and put away. Percy was exhausted.

Little noise emanated from the back room while she worked in the kitchen. Every so often she would hear the shuffle of Joshua's feet as he moved across the room and checked on Troy more closely. She had taken them food while the men ate. Troy was too weak to sit up for very long, but he ate hungrily and gratefully before dropping off to sleep again. Now Percy remembered that she had not gone back in to collect their dishes. Wiping her hands on her apron, she entered her bedroom-turned-clinic.

"I came for the dishes," she said softly, picking them up.

"I'm sorry," Josh responded. His haggard face showed the strain of the day. "I should have brought them out to you. I guess I dozed off myself."

"It's no problem. But I finished all the others, so I think I'll leave these till the morning."

"The biscuits were superb. I can see why the men like your cooking."

"Thank you."

"Troy is sleeping soundly. When you get your things together, I'll walk you over to Lacey's house."

"That's not necessary. I can manage."

"I'd like to do it."

Percy started to protest further, but stopped. He was looking

89

at her with his clear, honest brown eyes and she believed him. "All right. I'll just be a few minutes."

Percy left the dishes in the sink, soaking, and tried to focus on what she would need overnight at Lacey's house. Opening up her trunk and extracting a nightgown and other personal items was awkward, although Josh discreetly kept his eyes turned in another direction. Percy quickly picked up a clean dress—she still wore the blood-soaked one—and her hairbrush, stuffed everything in a pillowcase, and announced she was ready to go.

Josh stood up wearily.

"You really should stay here," Percy said. "You're dead on your feet. Anyone can see that."

"The fresh air and a few moments of exercise will do me good," Josh said.

"Where are you going to sleep? I haven't got any other bedding to offer you."

"Remember the army cot on Lacey's back porch? I think there's room to squeeze it in here for the night."

Ah, so that was it, Percy thought. He hadn't really wanted to walk me down the street. He just wanted a cot. She swallowed the tart reply that leaped to her mind.

After a last glance at Troy, they left through the front door. The night was warm and sticky, as were all the nights now. But the sky was cloudless and glistened with the light of the galaxy.

"Look at that sky," Percy said amiably. If he insisted on walking her down the street, she might as well make the best of it.

"It's pretty amazing," Josh agreed. "Even more amazing is the thought that the Maker of that sky was in your bedroom today."

Percy looked at him sharply. "Are you talking about God?"

Josh was amused. "Do you know someone else who could make a night like this?"

Percy did not respond. She had been taught to believe that

God made heaven and earth, and she supposed she did believe that. But that God would be involved in what had happened that day was beyond acceptance.

"I can imagine that looking after Troy was not an easy thing for you to do," Joshua said gently. "He's been openly hostile toward you more than once, and he can be quite a troublemaker. Yet you took him in and cared for him."

"I didn't have much choice," Percy said abruptly. "Peter and Travis insisted on carrying him in there. And you insisted that I stay and pretend to be a nurse."

"You did very well," Josh said, smiling in the dark. "You could have just walked away and refused to help."

"The thought did occur to me," Percy admitted.

"You might have even thought that Troy Wilger got just what he deserved," Josh said.

Percy did not want to admit aloud that she had thought that exactly when she first saw who the wounded man was. "He does seem to be more trouble than he's worth sometimes," she said cautiously. "Travis and Peter seem to be quite indulgent of behavior that many would find unacceptable. For some reason, they must think he's worth all the trouble he causes."

Josh paused a moment before responding. "Aren't we all more trouble than we're worth? By God's grace, people put up with us, even love us sometimes."

Not me, Percy thought. *I have to earn my way every step that I take. I don't ask for an ounce of anyone's grace, much less God's.* Aloud, she said, "I prefer to believe that I don't go around causing chaos and havoc everywhere I go."

Josh laughed. "I would say that your mere arrival here a few weeks ago caused considerable chaos and havoc."

Percy was glad the night hid her blush. "Don't misconstrue my words. That's not the same thing at all. I'm not anything like Troy Wilger. And neither are you."

"At some level, we all are," Josh said softly. "But thankfully, that's not the end of the story."

Percy wanted to continue her adamant protest against a

comparison between her and Troy Wilger, but they had arrived at the Gates house. She pressed her lips together to compose herself and told herself she should have brought the pie still sitting in her kitchen. It might have made coming over here under these circumstances less awkward.

"Lacey and Travis will still be up," Joshua said confidently as they started up the front porch steps. "I'm sure by now Travis has explained to Lacey why you didn't show up with the pie this afternoon."

Lacey was in fact still up, reading by lamplight in the living room. She welcomed them warmly and listened with rapt attention to the report that Joshua gave on Troy's condition.

"Thank God he's going to be all right," Lacey said when Josh finished. "And thank God that you were there, Josh. Even just last year, he would have had to be taken south and the trip might have killed him. And Percy, thank you for staying to help Josh. Don't worry about what you missed this afternoon. We'll do it again soon."

"It may be a few days before I can move Troy," Josh explained to his sister. "I'm going to take the cot and stay over there with him. Percy can stay in my room, if that's all right with you."

"Of course it's all right. I'll go up now and change the bedding."

"Don't go to all that trouble," Percy protested. "If you give me the sheets, I'll change them."

"Don't be silly. You're my guest. Sit down and relax. There's tea on the stove if you want it."

Lacey flew into action and armed Josh with a pillow and blanket to go with his cot, and she had changed the sheets on Josh's bed before Percy knew what had happened. It seemed like only a few minutes later that Percy found herself standing in the middle of Joshua Wells's room, with the bed invitingly turned down and a lamp glowing softly on the nightstand. On top of the dresser Lacey had left a wash basin of steaming water. Percy glanced down at herself and began to peel the soiled dress off. Grateful for Lacey's thoughtfulness, she scrubbed her face and arms. By the time she pulled her night-gown over her head, she felt almost refreshed. She turned around to survey the room more carefully.

Percy had not seen this room on her previous visit to the house. By most standards, it was not a large room, but compared to her own quarters, it was enormous. The double-sized bed had a thick, lofty mattress and was covered by an intricate, colorful quilt. Percy wondered if the quilt was the handiwork of Lacey or her mother. A small bookcase in one corner held a range of medical books and another stack sat on the desk across from the bed. A plain pine wardrobe no doubt held the simple collection of clothing that belonged to Dr. Wells.

Josh kept his room neat, Percy concluded. Lacey had hardly been up here long enough to change the bedding, much less straighten up the room. No, Josh was orderly and thoughtful in private, just as he appeared around other people.

Percy sat on the edge of the bed and let out an involuntary squeal. It was softer than anything she had slept on for years, ever since. . . She refused to let her mind conjure up the picture of her childhood bed and the reason she had left it behind. But a moment of envy told her it would be difficult to go back to her own bed after a few nights here. She pulled her legs up from the floor and curled them under her in the softness. From her comfortable spot, Percy examined the nightstand. Another stack of medical books made her smile. Joshua surely was absorbed by his profession, even as limited as his practice was. Then she saw the Bible. It looked well thumbed and familiar, like her grandmother's Bible looked. So he was serious about that, too, Percy said to herself. Well, if he had lived the life she had lived, maybe he would have a different perspective.

She picked up the leather volume, not unlike her grandmother's Bible. It seemed to fall open naturally to the middle, to Psalm 27:1: "The Lord is my light and my salvation; whom shall I fear? the Lord is the strength of my life; of whom shall I be afraid?"

Percy read no further. She was afraid, even if she admitted it to no one but herself. But for this one night, perhaps she could feel safe. She turned away from the Bible and let herself sink into the glorious oblivion of the featherbed.

fifteen

Percy soon grew afraid that she would become too accustomed to the comforts of Joshua's room and Lacey's home. The bed was soft, the sheets clean and cool, the quilt an obvious heirloom.

She awoke the first morning well rested from sleeping in the spacious featherbed. In the haze of the early morning consciousness, for a moment she thought she was in her old bed, the one in the room with the wallpaper of neat rows of tiny blue flowers. She expected to open her eyes and see the eyelet curtains and the breakfast tray with tea and toast. But the confused memory lasted only a second. Percy jolted to full consciousness and bolted out of bed, sure that she had overslept. She darted across the room and threw back the plaid cotton—not white eyelet—curtains and judged the sun. Her heart slowed its pounding. She was not late. If anything, she had awakened early. Swiftly and quietly, she dressed and left the house.

At the end of the day, Joshua insisted that Troy, although much improved, was not ready to be moved. And there was no place to move him to anyway. As diplomatically as he could, Josh impressed upon Percy that her quarters would have to serve as the infirmary until Troy was strong enough to rest on his own in the bunkhouse. Josh would not predict how soon that might be, so Percy returned to the Gates house for another night. It was nearly bedtime for the Gates boys by the time Percy arrived, but Adam successfully pleaded permission for one game of checkers.

"Grandpa is coming tomorrow," Adam announced.

"Oh?" Percy responded as she slid her checker closer to Adam's side of the board.

"He's coming for lunch," Adam explained. "Why don't you have lunch with us, too?"

Lacey interjected immediately. "That's a wonderful idea. Take a break from that garden of yours and enjoy a meal that you didn't have to cook."

"Oh, I don't know. I wouldn't want to get in the way of a family visit."

"Nonsense," Lacey insisted. "Papa wants to meet you, anyway. We've been telling him stories."

Percy smiled awkwardly, embarrassed. "I hate to think I've done anything worth telling stories on."

"My father is easily entertained," Lacey said.

And so Percy found herself at the Gates house for lunch the next day. Lacey prepared a menu that would appeal on a hot day: a fruit tray, bread with cheese and jam, and cool tea poured over ice chipped off the block in the icehouse.

"Oranges!" Percy exclaimed. "Where did you get oranges from?"

"Travis brought back a dozen from his last trip. I'm sure he would have brought six dozen for you if he had been able to get them."

"I'll just enjoy a few orange slices here and not mention to any of the men that I had them."

"Thank you for your discretion," Lacey said amiably.

"Can I help you set the table?"

"Thank you. There's a clean tablecloth hung over the back of that chair."

Percy hardly finished laying out the dishes before the front door swung open. Adam and Caleb heard the familiar creak and tumbled down the stairs and into their grandfather's arms. Daniel Wells feigned weakness, collapsed to his knees, and allowed them to knock him over. Giggling, Caleb positioned himself squarely on his grandpa's chest. From his prostrate position, Daniel grinned up at the triumphant little boy.

"My turn, my turn," Adam demanded as he straddled his grandfather and nudged Caleb out of the way.

Watching the scene from across the room, Percy asked Lacey, "How often does your father come to visit?"

"About once a month," Lacey answered. "In between, we go over there. The trail has become so well worn over the years that it is a much easier walk than it used to be."

"It's several miles to the lighthouse, isn't it?"

Lacey nodded. "Several miles to a whole different world."

"What do you mean?"

"When Josh and I were little, the lighthouse was all we knew. We could roam for miles and not see anyone but our family for months at a time. Then the lumber camp came in. Abby's family moved in and things began to change. Twenty years ago no one would have guessed that there would be an argument about forming a town government here."

Daniel Wells drew himself to his feet, with one squealing boy wrapped around each leg. "Is that argument still going on?" he asked.

"It gets more animated all the time," Lacey said. "Josh is taking care of someone who was hurt in an accident with the saw, but Travis thinks there may be more to it than that."

"I'm sorry to hear that," Daniel said genuinely. "I know as well as anyone how difficult change can be, but fighting about it doesn't help anything." He lifted his eyes to Percy. "You must be the Miss Morgan I have heard so much about. One of the nicest changes I've seen in the camp in a long time."

"Thank you, Mr. Wells."

Gently shedding the boys, Daniel crossed the room and kissed Lacey's cheek. "We haven't had one of our talks on the lighthouse balcony for a long time. I miss that."

"Mmmm," Lacey agreed, smiling pleasantly, "I do, too. Next time I come over, let's ask Micah to take the boys out in the meadow to look for deer, and we'll go up the lighthouse."

"Don't wait too long," Daniel said. "I know how you sometimes let things build up inside you."

Percy felt a lump in her throat swell. Was this caring, gentle man really Lacey and Joshua's father? He seemed to know his daughter well. Percy could not imagine ever having a conversation like this one with her father, Archibald Morgan. He would never have known if her feelings were pent up inside her. He barely noticed whether she was in the house or not. He preferred not to engage in conversation outside of his study, and children were strongly discouraged from entering the room where he withdrew to brood. Daniel Wells did not hesitate to speak to the point. Percy could remember being thoroughly confused about what her own father was thinking. She was never even sure that he actually liked Percy or her younger sister. What they did or did not do with their pent-up emotions was certainly no concern of his.

"I'm not holding anything in, Papa," Lacey assured her father. "I'm quite happy. I promise you."

"Good. I'm glad to hear it. Now let's have that lunch before your sons tackle me and tie me to a post."

That was all the cue they needed. Adam gasped. "Caleb, let's find some rope!" And they were off.

Percy watched, wide-eyed. Was he serious? Was Daniel Wells really going to allow his grandsons to tie him up? She had never thought much about what kind of grandfather her own father might be, but she was certain he would not surrender to the ropes of two little boys. As it was, though, she doubted she would ever find out what sort of grandfather her father might be. She seriously questioned whether she would ever have the opportunity to have children of her own. And, of course, she had no idea where to find her father, even if she wanted to. His unknown whereabouts were not a problem, though, since Percy could not imagine the circumstances under which she would want to see her father again. After what he had done, what would be the point? No matter what her mind told her, though, Percy could not quite dissolve the lump in her throat as she watched Daniel Wells with his grandsons.

"I hear you are quite the checkers player," Daniel said to Percy. "Perhaps after lunch we can have a game. But you'll have to let Adam be my special consultant."

Percy fought for words. "I'd be honored. Certainly, we'll have a game. Caleb can be on my side." Archibald Morgan would never have suggested a game of checkers, much less agreed to take on a small child as a teammate.

"I'll get the food," Lacey said.

"I'll help," Percy added hastily, for she did not want anyone to see the mist that filled her eyes.

sixteen

Troy Wilger's health improved, but his attitude did not. For four days he occupied Percy's room, grumbling nearly every moment that he was conscious. When Lacey sent over clean sheets, Troy wanted nothing to do with them, even though he had been sweating and twisting in the bed for two days and the bedclothes were so damp and tangled he could hardly find a loose end on which to pull. When Percy heated water for Josh to give Troy a sponge bath, Troy nearly knocked the basin from her hands. It was all Josh could do to keep Troy in bed and resting. Troy repeatedly muttered about his wounded dignity and refused to accept the seriousness of his injury. Josh hardly dared leave the bedside for fear that Troy would try to get out of bed and demand his independence—and rip open his wound. And, of course, Troy had nothing pleasant to say about Percy, even as he commandeered her room and devoured the plates of food that she dutifully carried in at regular intervals. Each time Percy recalled that Josh had compared her to Troy, saying that at some level everyone was as much trouble as that hateful lumberjack, she was infuriated anew. Some day, she determined, she was going to challenge Dr. Joshua Wells on that remark and set him straight.

Percy occupied Josh's room for each of the four nights that Troy was in her room. Lacey kept a pot of coffee hot so that when Percy arrived in the evening they could sit together and relax for a few minutes. On the third evening, as they tidied Lacey's kitchen after drinking their coffee, Percy's heart caught in her throat. Lacey was no longer treating her as a guest but as a friend. Despite her city background, precious little friendship had ever graced Percy's life, unless she counted the brief attachment she had had to the gardener's

100

daughter. She hardly knew how to respond to Lacey's gracious informality.

On the last evening, Adam and Caleb got into a frightful scrap that made Percy's childhood arguments with Ashley, her younger sister, seem like polite conversation. But Lacey responded with firmness and authority, and the boys soon restrained themselves. Even a flare-up of sibling rivalry reminded Percy how different this home was from the one in which she grew up. Her own mother would have looked helplessly at the governess to resolve the conflict. Fortunately, her disagreements with Ashley had been rare. Their shared intuition about the tenuousness of their family's relationships bound them together in a silent pact. Also, Ashley was so much younger than Percy and they had very little over which to compete.

After watching Lacey discipline her sons, Percy went to bed with a heavy heart. *Will I ever have another chance to soothe Ashley?* She wanted to so badly, but it seemed a hopeless dream.

❧

Percy was relieved when Josh informed her that he was moving Troy to the bunkhouse and arranging for a rotation of people to take care of him. Troy was out of immediate danger, but he had to be watched or he would do something foolish and find himself under Josh's unrelenting eye once again.

Josh had done his best to keep Percy's small room tidy. After living in his immaculate room for four nights, Percy expected nothing else of him. He removed his army cot and replaced her trunk along the wall, and repositioned the side chair and nightstand, which he had been using as a table for his own meals. The room looked as it usually did. Still, Percy felt compelled to scrub everything in sight. She remembered in too much detail the scene of Troy's arrival: the streaming blood, the anguish on the faces of Travis and Peter, the enormous knot in her own stomach that nearly immobilized her. Scrubbing would make the room clean again and, more importantly, it would make the room hers again.

As modest and lonely as the room was compared to the warmth of the Gates home, Percy was relieved to be on her own again. She could easily imagine living among the physical comforts of Lacey's home. After all, while the Gates house seemed quite sophisticated for the lumber community, it was modest compared to the Morgan family home. Percy had no altruistic determination to live under harsh conditions for the rest of her life. Yes, she could imagine and even welcome the physical comforts of a real home. It was the less tangible dimension of the Gates home that would overwhelm her if she were not careful. Could such an atmosphere be true and lasting? She doubted it. So it was better, much better, that she was in her own room once again. Here there was nothing to trigger the memories of her own childhood, nothing to remind her how she had come to live under such curious circumstances in the first place.

She also welcomed the return of her demanding routine. Travis still had not found anyone willing to work with her in the kitchen and garden, but Percy was determined not to relax her ambitions. No matter how physically taxing, she would have a vegetable garden and a clean, well-operated kitchen.

On the fifth day after the accident, Percy set about taking inventory of her supplies and planning menus for the next week or so. She had a craving for potato soup, and she had been hoarding tinned milk for weeks in order to have enough to make a hearty, thick soup. With enthusiasm and a quick step, she crossed the kitchen and opened the cupboard door. Her taste buds were already savoring the soup. She would serve the men and clean up and then sit in the peace and quiet of the mess hall with her own evening meal. Percy reached into the cupboard. Her hands found the tins, but the pile did not feel right. Surely the stack should be taller! Puzzled, she peered into the cupboard—probably one-third of the cans of milk were missing. She had counted them just two days ago and was certain there was enough for the potato soup.

Percy frowned as she turned away from the cupboard. She had taken meals to Josh and Troy regularly and offered extra food in between meals, for which Josh had seemed grateful. Josh should have had no reason to raid her cupboard. Besides, he could not possibly have had use for so much tinned milk.

Curious now, Percy opened another cupboard door. The supply of beef jerky that she sometimes used in the packed lunches was there but, like the milk, it was considerably diminished. Again she told herself that Joshua could not possibly have consumed the quantity of food that was missing. But who would have? If some of the men were sneaking into the kitchen and removing food, she would have to ask Travis to put a stop to it. She planned her meals carefully, making the most of the supplies available, and she simply could not have people coming and fixing themselves snacks whenever they wanted to. Why would such a problem begin now, she wondered. Perhaps it was because people knew that she was not staying in the building at night. But they knew Josh was there, and certainly the men would not think he would approve of their stealing food.

Percy pressed her lips together in a hunch. Outside, in the back of the building, was an outside entrance to the cellar. She kept the potatoes down there in the cool darkness. Surely someone looking for a snack would not raid the potato stash. There was no way to cook them in the bunkhouse, although Percy supposed that anyone could go off into the woods, build a small fire, and roast potatoes.

Taking a burlap sack with her, she went outside to the cellar doors and pulled them open. The cellar was dark and, as always, it took a few minutes for Percy to be able to see when she descended. She was careful that the doors remained wide open behind her. Enough light filtered down the rough stairway that she knew she would be able to gather potatoes as soon as her eyes adjusted to the dimness, so she did not bother with lighting a lamp. The potato supply was substantial. Travis had found a good source and bought a wagonload of potatoes.

Percy had portioned them out so that most of the potatoes were at the rear of the large cellar, while a smaller pile was handy at the bottom of the stairs.

While she waited for her eyes to adjust, Percy studied the shadows at the back of the cellar. Something looked different, darker than usual, but she could not quite decide just what was different. Out of habit, she reached down for the potatoes, expecting to easily fill her bag. She stopped almost immediately. The pile was far too small. Percy was positive that quite a few potatoes were missing.

Pensively, she began dropping potatoes into the sack. *Something is wrong. What is it?*

She turned and peered into the grayness of the cellar and a shadow at the back of the cellar moved. It was almost imperceptible, but Percy was sure she had seen something.

"Who's there?" Percy demanded. She dropped her sack and reached for the broom that she kept parked against the wall.

The shadow rushed past her, nearly knocking her down in the rush up the stairs.

Percy scrambled to regain her balance and began the chase. No one was going to raid her cellar and get away with it that easily. She charged up the stairs, only steps behind the intruder.

In the open sunlight, the trespasser broke into a sprint across the uncluttered land behind the mess hall. Waving her broomstick, Percy chased him as hard as she could. He clutched a bundle to his chest as he ran. Whoever he was, he really was stealing her food.

Out of breath and outdistanced, Percy finally had to give up. He had gotten away and she had not recognized him. He was not one of the lumberjacks. He was young, probably not more than fifteen, she judged, and skinny as a rail. She turned back to the cellar. This time she paused to light a lamp on the ledge just inside the door and carried it down the stairs.

Percy looked around carefully for she knew exactly what ought to be in the cellar. Two jars of green beans were missing and some cherries she was saving for pies were gone. An apple core gave evidence that the thief had been too hungry to wait until he carried off his loot.

Percy could not imagine who the boy was, but she could remember, painfully, doing something not so different herself when her survival was in question. Whoever he was, he was desperate.

seventeen

After that, Percy watched her provisions carefully and wondered how long it would take to get a lock on the cellar door if she decided that she needed one. She had seen with her own eyes that there was an intruder, but she hoped that being discovered would frighten him off. On the other hand, discovery had not always deterred her when she had done the same thing. It only made her quicker and more sly. She was not proud of those days, but at least they had not lasted long—only for a few weeks after Ashley was gone and Percy had struck out on her own. She always hated the thought of stealing anything and, after what her father had done and the way the family had been treated, Percy had wanted nothing more than to prove everyone wrong. Desperately, she had hoped for an alternative to the cunning schemes that had flooded her mind, but none had come. For those few weeks, she had succumbed to something she hated. Perhaps the boy she had seen was not so different.

Lacey came to help in Percy's garden, after having spent much of the morning working in her own patch. Seeds had sprouted, their delicate leafy greens a testimony to the life and nourishment that they would bear. Some days when there was not much work that really needed to be done in the garden, Percy would simply sit among the plants and dream of the day when her labors would yield a lush harvest. On the day of Lacey's visit, they pulled out the random small weeds that had survived the tilling process and sprung up once again.

"Judging from the number of green beans you planted," Lacey said with a twinkle in her eye, "you must have quite a few recipes that require them."

Percy chuckled. "I may have gotten carried away."

"We'll find out when canning time comes."

"I know even less about canning than I do about gardening," Percy admitted.

"I suspected as much," Lacey said. "But you're a quick learner. You seem to pick up whatever you put your mind to."

Percy did not answer. She was thinking, *If only you knew how much I've had to learn.* But she could not tell Lacey.

"Josh was asking about you the other day," Lacey said.

"Oh?"

"He wondered if you were comfortable while you were staying with us."

"I hope you assured him that I was quite spoiled."

"He would only say that you deserved to be spoiled."

"He would?" Percy was stunned.

"I believe I know my brother quite well," Lacey said, her lips twisting mysteriously to one side, "and I would have to say that he seems to have a particular regard for Miss Percy Morgan."

Percy blushed. "Don't be silly. I've never given him any encouragement."

"Is that what city girls are taught to say when a man shows an interest?"

"No. . .I mean, I don't know. Josh doesn't. . . What makes you say. . .?" As hard as she struggled, Percy did not seem able to complete a single sentence because what Lacey was inferring took her completely by surprise. Finally, she managed to say, "Can we talk about something else?"

"Sure. You choose the subject." Lacey said, hiding her smile and lowering her head to concentrate on a weed.

"Someone has been stealing from my provisions," Percy said abruptly.

Lacey's head snapped up. "Have you told Travis?"

Percy shook her head. "I will if I have to, but the boy might not come back."

"Boy? Not one of the lumberjacks?"

Again, Percy shook her head. "I'd never seen this boy

before. He's young, probably younger than your brother Micah, and skinny as a rail. I thought maybe you would know him."

"What did he look like?"

Percy shrugged. "Brown hair, I think. I didn't really get a look at his face. I caught him in the cellar and it was too dark to see him well. He ran out ahead of me, so I saw only his back."

"Which way did he go?"

Percy pointed into the woods. "That way."

"Mmmm," Lacey said thoughtfully. "I suppose he just took off in whatever direction would get him away from you without drawing attention to himself. I can't imagine who it is. Josh hasn't mentioned any families up this way, but we could ask him. He might know."

"Whoever he is, he took several jars of beans, so I may need the ones I've planted."

"What was that?" Lacey asked, looking up and scanning the back of the mess hall.

"What was what?" Percy followed Lacey's gaze.

"I saw something."

"A person?"

"No, not a person. But a shadow."

"Are you sure?"

"Positive." Lacey rose to her feet and brushed the dirt off her hands. "I want to investigate."

"Do you think it might be the thief?"

Lacey scrunched up her face. "If it is, he's not a very smart thief. Coming back here in broad daylight is asking to be discovered."

They peered at the back of the building but nothing stirred.

Percy was on her feet now, standing beside Lacey. "Are you sure you saw something?"

"Absolutely," Lacey insisted. Suddenly she lunged forward. "There it is again." She broke into a trot and Percy stumbled through the dirt after her. Lacey kept her eyes fixed on what she had seen. "You go around that way," she said to Percy, pointing to the far side of the mess hall. "Don't let him run out into the street." Lacey was in a full run now.

This time Percy had no broom handle in her hands and she wondered what she would do if she did come face to face with the thief. Nevertheless, she followed Lacey's instruction and she cut around to the other side of the building, glancing around for a weapon as she ran. Just as she rounded the corner at the front of the building, she snatched up the biggest rock she could spot in the dirt. She was fairly confident she could raise it and strike with one hand if necessary.

The boy was pressed up against the front of the building, his face blanched and his lower lip quivering almost imperceptibly. Percy lowered her stone for he was no threat to her.

"I've caught him," Percy called out as Lacey rounded the other side of the building.

"Is it the same boy?" Lacey called back.

At the sound of her voice, the boy wheeled around and faced Lacey. He said nothing. From behind him, Percy saw his shoulders rise and fall with rapid breath.

Lacey stopped in her tracks. "TJ?"

The boy nodded.

Percy came up close behind him to face Lacey. "Do you know him?" she asked, incredulous.

Lacey nodded. "This is TJ Richards. He was once a student of mine."

"I hope that not all of your students have turned out to be thieves." Percy regretted her words as soon as she spoke them, but they were already out. *How many times have I endured such comments about myself?*

Lacey stepped forward to embrace TJ. "I'm sure there's an explanation."

TJ returned the embrace wholeheartedly. He spoke for the first time. "I've been watching you. I wanted to be sure it was really you."

With one arm around TJ's shoulders, Lacey turned toward

the door. "Percy, let's go inside and give this boy a decent meal while he tells us why he is stealing your green beans and potatoes."

TJ ate with gusto everything that Percy put in front of him. He was pitifully thin and bony. She opened one of her precious tins of milk and let him have the whole thing, along with some ham and biscuits left over from breakfast.

"It's been eight years," Lacey said. "That would make you sixteen now. I remember that you were the same age as my youngest brother, Micah."

Percy could hardly believe the boys were the same age. Though slight of build himself, Micah was far more robust.

As he consumed the last of the ham, Lacey spoke gently. "TJ, tell us why you're here. Somehow I don't think this was an accident."

He shook his head. "No, it's not an accident. I came looking for you."

"How did you find me?"

"I've been studying maps of Wisconsin for a year or more. I remember all the stories you used to tell us about growing up in the lighthouse and the dangers of the lake."

"Why have you come?" Lacey asked softly. "Your father?"

TJ grimaced. "He doesn't know where we are."

"We? You mean—"

"Sally and Mama are with me," he said simply.

"You've been stealing food to feed your family?"

He nodded. "I remember the day you found me hiding while my daddy was drunk. You wanted to take me home with you."

"I remember. You wouldn't come because you thought he would start in on your sister if you left, and you didn't want to take Sally away and break your mother's heart."

"You told me that day that you figured I was God's business. I never forgot that. And you said that God had made me your business, too."

Lacey nodded. "I remember." She turned to Percy. "TJ's

father drinks nearly all the time, and when he's drunk he beats up on TJ. But TJ didn't want to leave and put his mother and sister in danger."

"I can take care of them now," TJ said. "I'm older and bigger. I can get a job and support them, and I can stand up to my daddy if I have to."

"How did you convince your mother to leave? I didn't think she ever would."

"She didn't want to at first," he admitted. "But I told her I was taking Sally, and she would have to choose between Sally and Daddy."

"She chose Sally."

He nodded. "I saved and planned for months. She knew I would really do it."

"Where are your mother and sister?" Lacey asked urgently.

"In the woods. We have a place there."

"A place?" Lacey asked skeptically.

"We brought a piece of canvas with us, and we have some rope. I made us a tent."

Lacey stood up. "We must go get them and bring you all here immediately. I won't have you living in the woods for a moment longer."

eighteen

Lacey meant business. "The boys are at Abby's. Give me a minute to run down and tell her I'll be gone."

Before Percy could protest, she was left alone with TJ. He scraped his plate nervously.

"Do you want more to eat?" she asked.

"No, ma'am," he replied softly, not lifting his eyes.

"Are you sure? I have plenty more."

"Thank you, ma'am. I'm grateful for the meal."

"How long has it been since you've had a real meal?"

TJ blushed. "Well, my mama can do some amazing things with potatoes and a campfire. But I guess that's not the same as a real meal."

"Your mother and sister will be eating better before long, too."

TJ swallowed hard but said nothing.

"How long has it been since you left home?"

"We've been on the road about six weeks," TJ answered. His voice was barely audible. "But that place was never home to me. I aim to make a real home now. Even if it's just a piece of canvas in the woods, a home should be safe, a place where you know you belong."

Percy choked on the lump in her throat. This boy was barely sixteen years old, the age she had been when home as she knew it fell apart. But, to her envy, he had an understanding of what a home ought to be.

TJ cleared his throat. "I'm sorry about the food, ma'am." Now TJ lifted his sincere blue eyes and looked straight at Percy.

They are beautiful eyes, glowing islands of hope on a face of despair. Percy sighed. "It's all right."

"I knew it was wrong, and if I'd been on my own, just me, I mean, I wouldn't have done it. But my mama and Sally. . ."

Even when she was on her own, alone, Percy had snitched food. How could she judge TJ for wanting to feed his family? "Don't worry about it, TJ. You'll find a way to make it right." That's what she had done. Percy had never been caught like TJ, but she had wanted to make things right. She rose to clear his dishes from the table and her memories from her mind.

Lacey was back soon. "Let's go. TJ, lead the way."

Percy was speechless at Lacey's determination to help. No doubt her day was already full of other obligations, and what Lacey planned to do with three extra people Percy could not imagine. But she was throwing that all aside to offer solace to a family she had known for only a few months more than eight years ago.

"Are you coming?" Lacey asked Percy.

"Yes, of course," Percy quickly answered. Somehow that seemed to be the right answer. She could hardly believe that the thief who had raided her precious tinned milk had moved her so, but she was and she could not refuse him help. *How old is his sister,* she wondered as she thought of her own sister, Ashley, who would be thirteen now.

They went out the back door, crossed the garden, and were soon into the woods. TJ seemed confident about where he was going. He moved skillfully and silently along a path that was invisible to Percy. He meandered such that Percy would have been hard pressed to duplicate the route. Clearly he had been determined to stay hidden until this moment. Having found Lacey Wells Gates, he was ready for revelation.

"North and a little bit west," Lacey mused. "Are we headed to that spot with the big rocks? The three boulders that come together in a sort of triangle?"

TJ flashed a look of surprise, then relief. "I guess when you live your whole life in a place, you know all the ins and outs."

"I'm sure you knew every hiding place in Tyler Creek," Lacey said. "I found you in more than one, remember."

"I remember. And yes, we're going to the place where the boulders are. They give pretty good shelter, and we hung the canvas."

"You've spent your last night there, I promise you."

TJ looked at Lacey with more gratitude than Percy could imagine mustering. The truth was no one had ever given her reason to be that grateful. When she was sixteen and suddenly estranged from her upbringing, no one had offered her solace and shelter. How different might things have been if someone had. She would never know.

At least TJ knew where his sister was. He was doing his best to care for her and keep her safe. Percy had not been able to do that for Ashley. *Ashley!* her mind cried out. *I'm sorry!*

"Surely your father knows you're all gone by now," Lacey was saying. "Do you think he'll look for you?"

TJ shrugged. "I don't know. He'll be right angry, I'm sure, but I don't know if he cares enough to come looking."

"He might not care for you," Lacey said gently, "but he may be infuriated at having been tricked."

"I don't know if he can stay sober long enough to figure out where we went."

"But he might," said Lacey.

"Yes, ma'am, I suppose he might."

"And there are plenty of people in Tyler Creek who know where I came from."

"Yes, ma'am."

"We'll just have to be very careful, that's all. We won't let him find you."

"Yes, ma'am. Thank you, ma'am."

"We're almost there, aren't we?"

"Yes, ma'am." TJ paused. Percy and Lacey stood behind him.

Before them were the three boulders Lacey had described. They were perhaps eight feet tall and lopsided enough that they did indeed lean into each other. With the help of long sticks stuck in the ground, a worn piece of canvas was stretched over the opening in the midst of the boulders. Percy could see a small bundle tied to one of the makeshift poles and the evidence of a small campfire within a ring of small rocks. Three tin plates sat on the ground just outside the ring.

"I don't see them," Lacey said urgently.

"They probably heard us coming."

"So they're hiding?"

"Yes, ma'am."

"But we want to help, not hurt them!"

"Yes, ma'am. But I told them not to trust anyone, not until we found you."

"Will they come out if you call?"

TJ formed his lips to give a low, melodic whistle. It did not last long, but it was a distinct sound. The three of them stood motionless and watched. Slowly, two thin, weary forms appeared from behind the large boulder on the left.

"Sally!" Lacey called out as she began to move forward.

The smaller form lurched into a trot and headed directly for Lacey. "Miss Wells, is that really you?" Sally said as she threw herself into Lacey's arms.

"It's me, it's me." Lacey stroked the girl's head pressed against her shoulder.

Tears sprang to Percy's eyes. She judged the girl to be only a couple of years younger than TJ. She was small, but had the roundedness of young womanhood. Her long brown hair was matted and needed a serious cleaning and brushing. Her dress was patched in at least a half-dozen places and was clearly too short and too tight across the shoulders. The toes on her left foot showed through the flap that resulted from torn stitching. But seeing Sally Richards in Lacey's arms was a beautiful sight.

Percy's own arms ached to hold Ashley just that way. Would she ever be able to?

Lacey now opened her arms to Alvira Richards.

"I'm so sorry I wouldn't let you help us all those years ago," Alvira said, sobbing softly. "I know you meant only the best for us."

"Yes, I did," murmured Lacey, "and I still do. You're coming home with me, all of you. This time I'm going to do exactly what I wanted to do eight years ago. I don't always understand God's timing, but I'm glad he's given me another chance to care for you."

TJ smiled. "So you still think God made us your business?"

"More than ever. He brought you right to me! How could I think any differently?"

"I'm right grateful for your help," Alvira said, "but I'm mindful that the three of us can be a handful of trouble."

Lacey shook her head. "Don't worry. We'll figure it out. My boys can bunk in with their uncle, and you and Sally can have their room for the time being. We'll get TJ a job. I happen to have some influence with the man who does the hiring! You'll be on your feet before you know it."

Lacey turned her attention to the makeshift shelter and Percy took up the cue. "Let's get your things together," Percy said. "What can I carry?"

TJ looked at her sheepishly. "Well, ma'am, there are a few jars of green beans and a sack of potatoes. Perhaps you'd be interested in them."

Percy smiled broadly. "Yes, I would. And I would be especially interested in any tinned milk you might have lying around."

"Yes, ma'am, we have that, too."

nineteen

After breakfast the following day, Percy rushed through her cleanup routine, anxious to go back to Lacey's house and see what the next step would be for Alvira and her children. She wrapped a batch of fresh cinnamon rolls in a napkin, tucked them in a basket, and set off down the street.

"The lady from the street is here," Adam announced. "I think she wants to see the lady from the woods." Lacey, Alvira, TJ, and Sally were gathered around the kitchen table enjoying midmorning coffee.

Percy narrowed her eyes and glared playfully at Adam. To Adam she would always be the lady from the street.

"I'm glad you came over," Lacey said warmly as she pulled another chair up to the table for Percy. Caleb crawled up onto his mother's lap as she sat down again. "You can help us make a plan for how we're going to take care of our new friends."

Lacey spoke so easily of friendship. After trekking back to Lacey's house with the meager belongings of the Richards family, Percy had heard more of the story of Lacey's connection with TJ and his sister. Her stomach wrenched as she listened to the stories of drunkenness and beatings and how Bert Richards behaved in public as if he were the model father. The account reminded Percy of another father who was far different than he led people to think.

Percy turned to Alvira. "I hope you enjoyed sleeping in a real bed," she said, remembering the four luxurious nights she had under the Gateses' roof. She herself had spent the night wrestling with her memories and now hoped that her sleeplessness did not show in her face.

"I was afraid I wouldn't sleep a wink," Alvira said hesitantly, "what with all the excitement yesterday. I haven't been

117

sleepin' all that well lately, ever since. . . . But I slept like a well-fed baby."

"That's good to hear," Lacey said. "I intend for you to be fed well and to sleep well every night from now on."

"Perhaps these will help," Percy said, placing her basket of cinnamon rolls in the center of the table.

"You made these?" Sally said, her eyes wide. "Mama, these look just as good as yours."

Alvira laughed. "I don't suppose a body gets a job as a cook unless she can cook. If we eat those, we'll be headed for sweet dreams again tonight." She reached out to pinch off a piece of cinnamon roll.

"I don't remember the last time I slept as well as I did last night," Sally said, helping herself to an entire roll. "Maybe not in my whole life."

You slept because you felt safe, Percy thought. *I remember the weeks of not sleeping, of wondering how long I could stay where I was, the hungry, exhausting days.*

"It was right kind of your boys to give Sally and me their room," Alvira said to Lacey.

"Oh, it was nothing. I'm sure they thought it was great fun to bunk in with Uncle Josh. They've been talking about it all morning. The sofa may have been a bit uncomfortable for TJ, though."

"It's a whole might better than a mattress of pine needles," TJ responded brightly. Then he sobered. "But I know I can't sleep on your sofa permanently. I aim to get us a place to live as soon as possible."

"Around here that means building a place," Lacey informed him seriously. "There aren't any empty houses or abandoned farms like there might be down south."

"What did Travis say?" Percy asked, knowing that Lacey must have used her influence on her husband to try to better the lot of the Richards family.

"He promised to give TJ a job," Lacey said brightly. Then she laughed. "He wanted to assign TJ to work with you in the kitchen, but TJ wasn't sure he wanted to do that."

Percy glanced at the sheepish TJ. "No offense, ma'am. I ain't proud of what I did and I reckon I have some debt to work off in your kitchen. But I'm the man in the family now, and I aim to do a man's work."

"Am I really so frightening?" Percy teased. "I promise not to chase you with a broomstick again."

TJ blushed. "No, ma'am. It's just that I hiked all the way up here from Tyler Creek because I had my mind set on being a lumberjack."

"Then you should be a lumberjack," Percy agreed. *If only I had believed in myself that much when I was sixteen.*

Alvira said, "I'm proud to see my boy doing a man's work."

"From what I see, you have every reason to be proud of your boy," Percy said softly. Had anyone ever been proud of her? It seemed that every word spoken stirred up memories she thought she had long buried.

"Josh was about TJ's age when he started working in the camp," Lacey commented. "You might be sore for a while, TJ, while you build up your muscles, but I know you can do the job."

"TJ's right, though," Alvira said somberly. "We can't impose on your hospitality. Your boys may think it's fun to sleep with their uncle, but he might think different. A man deserves to have his home just the way he likes it."

Percy sighed. Her father certainly always had his home just the way he liked it. She hoped that Josh was somehow more congenial in the face of last night's invasion.

"Once TJ starts working," Lacey explained, "he can stay in the bunkhouse with the other men. You and Sally are welcome to stay here as long as you need to."

Alvira shook her head adamantly. "No, ma'am. You have a very big heart. I understand why my boy wanted to come all this way to find you. But we have to stand on our own feet."

"But there are no houses," Lacey protested.

"We have our canvas," Alvira said. "We'll find a place closer into town that we can pitch a tent."

Lacey chuckled "My husband would be pleased to hear you call this place a town."

"I remember when Tyler Creek wasn't much more than this."

"Mama," TJ said, "Tyler Creek is still just a speck of dirt on the map."

"Town or no town, I don't want you living under a piece of canvas," Lacey said insistently.

"Beggin' your pardon, ma'am, but we can't stay here," Alvira said, just as insistently. "It wouldn't be right."

"What about the shed?" Percy suggested.

"The shed?" Lacey echoed.

"Yes, the one behind the mess hall. It's got a few old tools in it and scraps of lumber. I never see anyone go in there."

"I'd almost forgotten it was there!" Lacey exclaimed. "But you're right. We could clean that place up and there would be plenty of room for a couple of cots."

"I'm going to build a real house," TJ said, "but it might be that this is the best we can do for now."

"A real house could take years to afford," Lacey said. "The shed will keep your mother and your sister out of the elements in the meantime. That was a good idea, Percy. And I have another one. Why not have Alvira work for you in the kitchen?"

Percy perked up. "Really?"

Lacey turned to Alvira. "What do you think? Sally says you can make cinnamon rolls as good as these. I'll bet you have a whole book of recipes in your head."

"Well," Alvira said reluctantly, "I reckon I do know how to cook. But I can't imagine getting paid to do it. I've never had no job."

"I've never had a job," Sally said, correcting her mother's grammar. "Miss Wells, I mean Mrs. Gates was our teacher. We should speak right."

"I'm glad you said that, Sally," Lacey said, "because that's the rest of my idea. Sally, I want you to finish your schooling. You're fourteen now, right?"

"Yes, ma'am."

"What grade were you in when you were last in school?"

"The sixth grade, ma'am."

Lacey pressed her lips together thoughtfully. "We'll have some catching up to do then. But we'll work on it. I want to see you get your eighth-grade certificate."

Sally's eyes lit up. "Really? You'd be my teacher again?"

"Absolutely. We'll start tomorrow, if you like. I'll listen to you read and see how your arithmetic is, and we'll make our plans from there."

Sally jumped out of her chair and threw her arms around Lacey, who was still holding Caleb.

"Hey!" Caleb protested the confinement of so many arms entangled around him.

Sally stepped back, laughing. "When we left home, I thought that was the end of school for me. I'll study hard, I promise. I'll be the best student you ever had."

Percy stood up awkwardly and moved toward the stove, acting as if she wanted a cup of coffee. She didn't, really, but she did not want anyone to see her face just then. How different the story would be for TJ and his family, compared to her own. She had longed for someone to merely speak a kind word to her, much less offer her housing and a job. But no one had. Week after week she heard only harsh words, blaming words, a tone that urged her to stop being such a bother as quickly as she could. She admired TJ's independence and fierceness because she understood it, and she knew exactly what would compel him to clear a path for his mother and sister.

Coffee cup in hand, she turned around and observed TJ from behind. If only she had been as successful in her own quest. If only someone had reached out to her with just one kind gesture when she was sixteen. Maybe things could have been different.

Ashley, her heart cried out, *I'm so sorry.*

twenty

Having Alvira's help changed Percy's life. The after-meal cleanup was done in a snap with Alvira, and sometimes Sally, too, helping. The garden, which had sprouted very nicely but now needed frequent weeding, was not so intimidating. Alvira seemed to know just what to do to keep the birds and insects away. Clearly she was experienced at raising her own vegetables and squeezing every ounce possible from the harvest. She hauled water for the wash, scrubbed the kitchen floor, gathered eggs. Every afternoon after her lessons were finished, Sally appeared to work beside her mother. Percy had to say very little in the way of instructions. Alvira proved to be a proficient cook, even with making fifty servings at a time. More than once in the two weeks since Alvira began working, Percy had awakened to find that Alvira had breakfast nearly ready and that Percy was free to doze for another thirty minutes. She hardly knew what to do with such a luxury. In more than eight years she had not truly been free to sleep as late as she wanted.

Two weeks and three days after finding Alvira in the woods, Percy woke to the smell of brewing coffee and sizzling bacon. She turned over and buried her face in the pillow once again, tempted to let Alvira handle the entire breakfast. She pictured the flapjacks Alvira would make, fluffier than her own. After weeks of being perpetually tired, Percy could almost rationalize sleeping later and letting Alvira take the brunt of the early morning work, but the thought was fleeting. Meals for the men were her responsibility and Alvira was there to assist her, not to coddle her. Without any further self-pity, Percy rose, freshened up with the water that had stood in the basin on her dresser overnight, and dressed in the soft gray dress that had become her favorite work dress. By the time she entered the kitchen, Alvira was mixing flapjack batter.

"I was just about to bring you some hot water when you came out," Alvira said.

Percy smiled. "Thank you, but it's been years since I had anyone to bring me hot water in the morning. I suppose I've given up the habit."

Alvira looked puzzled. "Don't you heat it for yourself? I've never had anyone bring it to me at all, least not regular."

Percy blushed and looked away. Why did she let such things slip out? "It was a long time ago. At this time of year, the water doesn't turn icy overnight, so I don't really mind. But it was sweet of you to think of me."

"Why don't you sit down here and let me put some breakfast in front of you? You can have the first of the flapjacks and eat while they're fresh. I don't think you eat nearly enough, for someone who cooks for a living."

Percy briefly considered her waistline. Her skirt still hung awkwardly, but not so badly as last year. The hard-earned weight she had lost when she first arrived had come back. If Alvira only knew how bad things had been at one point in time. She glanced at the bacon, tempted.

"Alvira, you're a wonderful help," she said, "but you must not overwork yourself. You're here to help me, not replace me. There is plenty of work for two." She reached for an apron and tied it over her gray dress.

Alvira turned several strips of bacon and added some new ones to the pan. "I'm so grateful for this job. I just want to be sure I do right by it."

"You're doing just fine. I don't know how I ever got along without you."

"It's my first job, you know. I never really had a job before."

"You don't have a thing to worry about. You're wonderfully competent at everything you put your hand to. I only wish I could have said that about my first job."

"A fine lady like you ought to be livin' in a nice house with folks to look after her," Alvira said. "I know what brought me here, but I can't quite fathom how you ended up here. I can tell you have more breedin' than most."

Percy took a stack of tin plates from the cupboard and set them on the rolling cart that she would later push into the main dining room. If she were to tell Alvira about her father and what had become of her family, her new friend might not think so much of her fine breeding.

"I suppose we all just do the best we can," Percy said casually. "Perhaps breeding has little to do with how we fare."

"I knew it!" Alvira's eyes lit up. "You are a lady of fine breedin' but something awful happened. That's what brought you here."

"I needed a job, and the camp needed a cook," Percy said flatly. "That's what brought me here."

Alvira turned back to the flapjack batter. She splattered a drop on the griddle to test the temperature; it sizzled appropriately.

"My TJ believes that God brought us here to find Miss Lacey. He's believed that ever since that day that she told him God had made it her business to look after him, even when no one else would stand up to Bert and his ways. Can't say that I argue with Him." She dropped a generous spoonful of batter on the blistering griddle. "It does seem that God made the way plain for us to find her again, and now look at us. Sally's back in school and TJ and me are workin'."

Alvira prattled on as she made one batch of flapjacks after another and Percy assembled plates, cups, and silverware on the rolling cart. There was no question that Alvira had blossomed during the last two weeks. She was beginning to gain needed weight, despite all her vigorous work, and her cheeks were almost rosy. Alvira talked more every day, making Percy think that she had bottled up her thoughts and feelings for years. Now nothing could keep everything that was in her from streaming out uncensored.

Percy remained guarded. It would be easy enough to be

caught up in Alvira's gushing. The story she told reminded Percy far too easily of her own. Alvira seemed not to mind if everyone knew the smallest details of her life. Years of being afraid of what others thought of her because of her husband faded quickly into a natural infectious gregariousness. Still, Percy chose her own words carefully.

After breakfast Josh appeared. Alvira was quick to offer him the last of the flapjacks and bacon. "I promised Lacey I would check up on you," Josh said to Alvira as she scurried around the kitchen. "If you would slow down a minute, I might like to check your pulse and have a look at your eyes."

Alvira waved him away. "I've never felt better in my life. I don't need doctorin'."

"You've been under a great deal of stress the last few weeks, what with leaving your home and the long journey up here. We have to be careful about your health."

Alvira set a plate down in front of Josh. She sobered suddenly. "No, you got that wrong. I was under a heavy burden before we ever left Tyler Creek. But it's been lifted away by folks like you."

Josh squeezed Alvira's hands. "We are but vessels of the One who bears your burden. God brought you to us, and we're grateful."

Alvira turned away to hide the tear in her eye. Percy swallowed the lump in her throat.

"How's that man you been tendin'?" Alvira asked.

"Troy Wilger? He's coming along nicely, actually. He should be able to go back to work in a few more weeks."

"Is he as cantankerous as ever?" Percy asked.

Josh smiled and nodded. "I'm afraid so."

"Someone always seems to come for his meals, so I haven't seen him in quite awhile."

"I'm sure he prefers it that way," Josh said. "He still bellows on and on about how much he hates progress. Some of the men have been referring to our little strip of buildings as 'town' and he hates that. We'll always be a camp in his mind."

"I don't see how it much matters what you call yourselves," Alvira said. "Camp or town, you're the folks that took me and my children in when we had no place to go. That's what matters, that you folks have tender hearts."

"That was beautifully put," Josh said. "Thank you, Alvira."

Alvira turned away, embarrassed. "I got chores to do."

"Alvira, take a short rest," Percy said. "You've been working for hours already."

"Not till the washing is hung," Alvira said. "I'm going to find the scrub board." And she left.

"Do you want any more to eat?" Percy asked. "We have a bit of cold bacon left."

Josh shook his head as his eyes followed her around the room. "How are you, Percy?" he asked. "Alvira is not the only person I wanted to check on."

"What do you mean?" Percy asked.

"We haven't seen much of you lately, and when I have seen you, you seem withdrawn."

"Do I?"

He nodded. "I was hoping Alvira's help would make things easier for you."

"It has, tremendously."

"Then why does it seem that you've gone deeper into your shell since she arrived? Alvira and Sally have been visiting in the evening, but Adam is wondering why the lady from the street doesn't have time for a game of checkers. I am, too."

Percy looked into Josh's dark, pondering eyes and nearly let go. Fleetingly, she wondered what it might feel like to tell her story, to unleash the stirrings within her.

"Tell Adam I'll come over soon." She avoided looking at Josh, moving instead toward the sink with his empty dishes.

"What shall I say when he asks why you have not come before now?"

She sighed. "It's a long story, Josh."

"My morning is unscheduled."

She looked at him again. If she could tell anyone, it would

be Josh. But no, she could not. She was on her own now and she had to stay that way. Telling him the truth would ruin everything.

Percy shook her head. "I'm sorry, Josh. Let's talk about something else. How is work on your clinic coming?"

Josh paused a long moment before answering. Percy pumped some water into the sink to cover the silence. "The lumber is piling up," he finally said, "and I believe we have agreed on a final version of the drawings."

"Will you have good living space?"

"I'll have two rooms in the back, a bedroom and a small sitting room, with space for a small kitchen. The front of the building will be a waiting room and an exam room, plus another bedroom for caring for patients who require an overnight stay. Peter's plans are drawn in a way that would make it easy to add on a second story later."

"It sounds like a very good arrangement," she said stiffly. She was sincere, but could not control her voice.

"I'm trying to convince Peter to use any scraps or cast off boards to help improve Alvira's situation."

"That's thoughtful of you. Perhaps he could build her something more adequate than the shed."

"That's what I'm hoping. It shouldn't have to cost a lot."

They conversed for another fifteen minutes. Percy could feel Josh's eyes on her the entire time, no matter where she moved about the room. Working hard to keep her tone light, she dared not look him in the eye for fear that her story would tumble out against her will.

twenty-one

"And after that," Percy said a week later as she and Alvira finished their midmorning coffee, "we should take an inventory of what is left in the cellar. Travis will be sending for supplies soon. We need to have a list ready."

They sat together in the vacated mess hall, their empty coffee cups on the table between them, along with evidence of blueberry muffins and a coveted orange.

"I've been thinkin' that—" Alvira did not get to finish her thought. Outside, a stack of lumber thundered to the ground, making them both start. Alvira gripped the edge of the table.

"That's the wood for Josh's clinic!" Percy said. She jumped up and scurried toward the window. "It was stacked next to the dining hall temporarily. I wonder what would make it fall."

"An animal, maybe," Alvira offered.

"I hope no one was hurt."

"Woman! Get out here!" bellowed a voice.

Percy stopped in her tracks, midway across the empty dining room.

Alvira gasped and jumped out of her chair. "It's Bert!"

"Your husband?" Percy was incredulous. "How did he find you?"

"I didn't think he could," Alvira said weakly. The color drained from her face. "We were careful and moved around every couple days till we got here."

"Are you sure that's him?"

Alvira nodded, her jaw clenched tight. "When you live with a man like that for twenty years, you know his voice even before he opens his mouth."

"Woman! Don't try to hide from me. I know you're here!"

"Nothing will stop him now," Alvira moaned. "I might as well go out there and spare everyone a lot of trouble."

"Don't you dare! You haven't come this far to give up that easily. He can't even be sure you're here."

"He might have spoken to one of the men out at the work site," Alvira said. "I just pray he didn't see TJ."

A multitude of scenarios flashed through Percy's mind. "TJ is safe as long as he stays with the other men. It's you I'm worried about. And Sally."

"Sally!" Alvira gasped anew. She began to run toward the front door.

Percy grasped Alvira's elbow as she flew past and stopped her. "You can't go out there," Percy said firmly.

"But Sally!" Alvira protested.

"We'll find her. She's at Lacey's for her lessons, isn't she?"

Alvira nodded mutely.

"Lacey won't let anything happen to her."

Outside, drunk and full of rage, Bert Richards kicked violently at the tumbled lumber, sending several planks clattering down the street. "I know she's here somewhere!" he shouted. "Bring me my woman!"

Motioning to Alvira to stay in the center of the large room, Percy moved stealthily toward a window on the front wall. If she ever wished there were curtains, it was now. She pressed herself against the wall and peered out into the street for her first glimpse of Bert Richards. He was about fifty, with gray-streaked brown hair that grew well beyond his collar and matched a beard that had never been trimmed. In one hand was a bottle, and he gulped greedily from it. When he had drained it, he smashed it to the ground.

"Woman!" he yelled.

Just then Travis and Josh emerged from the lumber office and, with confident strides, approached Bert. He took an angry swing, which Josh ducked.

Secretly relieved to see Josh but also anxious for him, Percy turned back to Alvira. She was determined that the frightened woman would not see her own fear. "Travis and Josh are out there. Let them try to talk to him. This is our chance to go out the back and go get Sally."

Alvira needed no further prompting; together they hurried across the dining room, through the kitchen, and out the back. Then they ran and in less than a minute, they arrived at Lacey's home and pushed open the back door.

Startled, Lacey looked up from the kitchen table where she was bent over a book with Sally.

"Your daddy's here," Alvira blurted out to her daughter.

Sally burst into tears.

Lacey pushed her chair back and jumped up. "Don't worry! We'll hide you!"

"Where?" Alvira asked weakly, bending to put her arms around the sobbing Sally. "He'll find us here sooner or later."

"But you won't be here. I sent the boys over to Abby's this morning so I could work with Sally. There's nothing to keep us from leaving right now." She slammed her textbook shut and took off her apron.

"Where are we going?" Sally asked, wiping her face with the back of one hand.

"To my father's. Bert won't find you there."

"What about our things?" Alvira asked.

"We can't worry about that now. We just have to get you out."

"I want to take my books," Sally said, having regained her composure. "I want to keep studying."

Percy looked at the thin girl with the big eyes. Three weeks of tutoring had changed her countenance. Fear had momentarily overtaken her, but Percy could still see the striking difference that lessons with Lacey had made. Sally's face exuded determination and perseverance.

Lacey nodded. "Yes, take your books. If you need anything else, I'll bring it to you later."

"Shouldn't we get horses?" Percy asked, imagining the long miles to the lighthouse.

"There's no time," Lacey responded. "We can't risk being seen."

She was right, of course.

"How long we gonna be there?" Alvira asked.

"As long as you need to be."

"With your pa? Alone?"

Percy saw the panic of scandal in Alvira's eyes. "Alvira, you have to keep yourself safe. You'll be safe with Mr. Wells."

"You won't be alone, Mama," Sally said. "I'll be there, and Miss Lacey's brother is there."

Alvira still looked uncertain.

"We have to get out of here," Lacey insisted. "I don't know how long Josh and Travis can hold him off. You must stay with my father and brother until we can manage something more suitable."

Mutely, Alvira nodded.

And they were out. They flew across the yard and found a trail. Years of trekking back and forth had taught Lacey every inch of the landscape. Now she guided the small entourage through the untrampled forest bed paralleling the main road but hidden from it.

Percy stumbled along behind the others, not sure why she was going—Sally and Alvira were safely in Lacey's care and there was little more Percy could do—but compelled nevertheless to go. Her feet tumbled along in an irregular rhythm. The group spoke little; all energy was focused on moving quickly and quietly through the forest, out of range of Bert Richards's raucous shouting. At the same time as she hoped in her heart for Alvira's safety, Percy hoped that it would not come at the expense of Josh or Travis. Had they been able to turn Bert away? Or had he harmed them and set off on a rampage through the woods?

When she caught sight of the lighthousè, Percy slowed her step for just a moment. Its majestic white, red-trimmed tower rising above the lake was just as Josh had described it once, and it beckoned to her now, calling her to safety, just as it beckoned to the ships that faced treacherous winter waters. Perhaps it meant that the story of Alvira and TJ and Sally would end in a better way than the story of Percy and Ashley and Myra had. Perhaps they would find the solace and refuge that Percy and her sister and mother had not found.

Long before they reached the house, the back door opened and Micah and Daniel Wells emerged and hurtled toward them. "What is it?" Daniel called when he was within shouting distance. "I can see that something is wrong."

"Papa, I need your help," Lacey said breathlessly as she allowed her father to embrace her. "This is my friend, Alvira, and her daughter, Sally. They need a safe place to stay."

Daniel nodded. "Joshua mentioned them when he was here last week. What's happened?"

"Bert's found the camp," Lacey said. "How he managed to track them here, I can't imagine, but he has. But he doesn't know where the lighthouse is. Maybe he doesn't remember that I came from here."

Micah relieved Sally of her burden of books. "If he shows up here, he'll have to get past Papa and me. And that won't be easy."

"I'm counting on that."

With tears in her eyes, Alvira looked at Daniel. "I'm a stranger and you're taking me in. How can I ever make it right with you?"

Daniel touched Alvira's shoulder gently. "There's no need to worry about that. Let's just pray that you're safe here."

Micah's mind was already figuring. "I'll move downstairs to Lacey's old room, and Alvira and Sally can have the big room upstairs."

"Oh, I hate to put anyone out," Alvira protested.

"I don't mind," Micah assured her. "It will be fun to have company in the house." He glanced sideways at Sally. "Especially someone near my own age."

Sally blushed but smiled. "Maybe we can study together.

Lacey says you're a good student. I'm having trouble with math."

"I'll help you." Micah fell into step with Sally and the two of them took the lead walking back toward the house.

They entered through the back door, and Percy found herself standing in the kitchen that Lacey and Josh had grown up in, looking at the table where Lacey had taken her lessons as a child. Through the doorway in the other room, she could see a piano and remembered that Joshua had reluctantly admitted that his mother had insisted that he learn to play. Above them rose the lighthouse. Josh had spoken to her of filling the lamps with whale oil, trimming the wicks, polishing the brass, shoveling coal into the kitchen stove, and hauling supplies up the side of the cliff every few months when the supply boat's owner remembered to come.

Lacey and Josh had not had a coddled childhood, not at all like Percy's. They had been isolated from a real community and expected to work hard from the time they were small children. Yet they had grown into adults who could open their hearts and take in a stranger and her daughter seeking safety. And Alvira and Sally were not the only strangers they had taken in, Percy reminded herself. They had taken her in, too.

twenty-two

A few hours later, TJ clattered into the dining hall. Percy had not been back very long herself. The waning afternoon had finally demanded that she return for the evening meal, and she and Lacey had traversed the trail once again. Percy now held a half-peeled potato in her hand, with one eye on the clock, wondering if she would make the mealtime deadline. She raised her eyes to meet TJ's when he entered the kitchen.

"I can't find Sally," he said. "I came to see if Mama knows where she is. I'm worried that she wandered off."

Percy set her knife on the edge of the sink and turned to face TJ.

"Your mother is not here, but Sally is safe," she said, wiping her hands on her apron. She spoke cautiously. "Have you been out at the work site all day?"

TJ nodded. "I just got back. I like to see Sally before supper, but she's not in the shed. It doesn't look like she's here, either."

"So you've been gone all day?" Percy verified.

"Miss Morgan, what's the matter?" Anxiety rose in TJ's voice. "Did something happen to Sally? Where's Mama?"

"Everything is fine. It's just that. . .your father was here this morning."

"Daddy? Here? How?" Percy saw the color drain from the boy's face as he asked the incredulous questions.

Percy gestured that TJ should sit at the small kitchen table and she quickly recounted what had happened in the street that morning.

"Where are Mama and Sally now?" TJ asked.

Percy hesitated. She and Lacey had agreed that it was best

134

if no one knew where Alvira and Sally had gone. "I have to ask you a question first," Percy finally said.

"Yes, ma'am."

"Do you want to go and stay with them?"

"Stay? You mean, give up my job?"

Percy nodded. "Temporarily. I'm sure Travis would take you back when it's safe."

TJ raised his roughened and calloused hands for inspection. "Finally my hands don't hurt every time I bend my fingers. Finally I'm earning some money to take care of my family. I can't quit now."

"I understand, and I think that's the right decision. But unless you want to go into hiding, I can't tell you where your mother and sister are. Lacey and I believe that it is safer for all of you if no one else knows."

"You have to tell me!"

She shook her head firmly. "No. You might try to go there. And what if your father is still lurking around in the woods watching you?"

"I'll be careful."

"I know you would be careful. But he managed to find you here when no one thought he would. We can't risk having him follow you."

"I won't go, I promise. I just want to know where they are."

Percy stood up and picked up her knife to resume peeling potatoes. "I'm sorry, TJ. I promised Lacey."

She looked at his crestfallen face and knew exactly how he felt. Nevertheless, she maintained her resolve. "You trust Lacey, don't you?"

He nodded. "More than anybody except God. She showed me how to trust God."

Percy was not sure what to make of that remark. She had learned from other people not to trust anyone. But she believed TJ.

"TJ, if you truly trust Lacey—and God—then you have to accept what I'm saying. Hopefully the separation won't last long. We just have to be sure your father has given up."

Heartbroken, TJ left a few minutes later when it was clear that pressing Percy further would yield no more information. Percy allowed herself to sink into a chair and slump her head down on the table. She hated denying TJ's request. In her mind's eye, she saw herself at an age not much older than he was, standing in her cousin's parlor, demanding to know where they had sent Ashley and no one would tell her. It was for Ashley's own good, they said. She had not believed them then, so how could she expect TJ to believe her when she said the same thing? If the look on his face was any indication, she was not sure that all his talk about trusting God would make any difference in the end. She hoped it would.

Somehow Percy muddled through the evening meal, avoiding TJ's eyes as he came through the serving line. He sat apart from the other men, ate quickly, and left. Acutely missing Alvira's company, she cleaned up after the meal and began laying out what she would need in the morning. When she heard footsteps crossing the main room, she intuitively grasped the handle of an iron skillet. The footsteps slowed on the other side of the door, in the darkened dining room. Percy tightened her grip.

"Who's there?" she called out.

The footsteps resumed, moving steadily closer.

"Who's there?" Percy demanded.

"It's me," came the soft voice of Joshua Wells, just as he pushed the swinging door open and stepped into the kitchen. He raised an eyebrow at the poised skillet.

"You should have come to the back door," Percy said brusquely, "so I could see it was you."

"You're quite right. I'm sorry if I frightened you. May I come in?"

Percy let out her breath and set the skillet down. Inwardly she was relieved to see him, to see for herself that Bert Richards had not harmed him. "Yes, of course. I have some coffee on the stove, if you'd like."

"That would be nice, if it's no trouble."

Percy moved to a cupboard and took down a cup and filled it. She set it in front of Josh, who had taken a seat at the table. "Is there something I can do for you?" she asked.

Josh caught her eyes and held her gaze. "I was wondering if I could do anything for you," he said gently. "You've had quite a day."

Percy ached to slump into a chair and weep, but instead she methodically pulled out a chair and lowered herself gracefully into it. "It has been an eventful day," she agreed. "Did Bert Richards hurt you this morning?"

Josh shook his head. "Not really. He was too drunk to throw a decent punch. It's amazing he ever found his way up here, as soused as he was."

"Apparently he has moments of sobriety during which he thinks quite clearly."

"It would seem that way. He stumbled around the street, banging on doors and screaming for Alvira. I was grateful than when we got here, you were gone. Thank you for taking Alvira out of here."

"It was the only thing to do. She's in a safe place now." Had Lacey told Josh where the refugees were? Percy wondered. She supposed that Josh might guess before long, but she resolved to say no more to Josh than she had to TJ.

"No one saw you leave," Josh said. "Travis was surprised to find Lacey gone when Bert headed toward the house. How four women managed to disappear together into the woods without being seen, I can't explain, but I'm glad you did. When we found Lacey and Sally gone, we knew you and Alvira were in safe hands, too."

"Lacey is the one who managed the whole escapade," Percy said. "I'm not even sure why I went along. I wasn't needed, not even to carry anything."

Josh shrugged. "There are different ways of being needed. I'm sure Alvira was glad you were there. She's become quite fond of you." He picked up his coffee cup and took a deep sip of the steaming liquid.

"Oh?" Percy was not sure how to respond. She stood up to pour herself some coffee, suddenly wishing to keep her hands busy.

"Anyway," Josh continued, "I just wanted to be sure you were all right."

"I'm fine, thank you." She seated herself at the table once again.

"You greeted me with a frying pan," Josh reminded her. "Are you sure you're all right? Do you feel safe here?"

"Considering Bert Richards's state of mind, I think a few prudent precautions are in order. How did you finally get him to leave?"

"He got even angrier when Travis would not let him near the house. He was just sure Lacey was hiding Alvira, and for all we knew, she could have been. But Travis stood his ground, and Peter had gone to his house to look after Abby and the children. So Richards was not getting anywhere. He cursed up a storm and finally left."

"Did he threaten to come back?"

Josh nodded. "I believe he will be back."

"Then it was wise of Lacey to take Alvira and Sally away."

"She wouldn't tell me where they are." Josh looked at her hopefully.

Percy smiled slyly. "Lacey and I made a pact, so you won't get anything out of me, either."

"Well, I have my suspicions."

Percy did not respond. She could not help if Josh's intuitions proved correct, but she would keep her word to Lacey and not be the one to tell him.

Josh pushed his chair back. "I suppose I should be going. I hate to leave you here, though."

"I'll be fine."

"It's not too late for a game of checkers over at the house."

"Adam will be in bed soon," Percy said.

"I wasn't thinking of inviting him to play," Josh said, catching her eyes. "I'll be happy to walk you back over here later."

Percy shifted her gaze. The pull to go with Josh to the Gates house was a strong one—too strong. She was not sure she could trust herself over there anymore, especially after a day as trying as this one. Surely she would say too much and regret it later. She shook her head.

"I really ought to stay here and get a few more things done. After all, I won't have Alvira in the morning and there was so much that didn't get done today."

"If I can't do anything for you tonight, I'm sure I can be of service in the morning." He stood up and moved toward the back door.

"That's not necessary. I managed on my own before Alvira came."

"I'm not offering because it's necessary, but because I want to. I'll see you bright and early."

He left before Percy could protest further. And she was not sure she wanted to protest further. She picked up the iron skillet and took it into the bedroom with her.

twenty-three

Each report that Lacey brought back from the lighthouse was more encouraging than the one before. Alvira was thriving, her cheeks rosier by the day and her countenance more serene. Daniel's garden kept her occupied and outdoors much of the time, but she did not neglect the indoors. Anxious to earn her room and board, she fastidiously cleaned every nook and cranny of the house, mended worn clothing, and polished the heirloom furniture until she could see Daniel's smiling reflection in every room. Sally, likewise, blossomed. With Micah to set a vigorous academic pace, she threw herself into her books more deeply than anyone could have imagined possible. Lacey temporarily excused Joshua from any visits to the lighthouse and went herself, every few days. Bringing new lessons for Sally, she could barely keep up with the rapid progress the girl made. Even Micah and Daniel seemed invigorated by the presence of their guests. Lacey reported to Percy that she had not seen her father so happy in years, and Micah seemed delighted to have someone in his own age bracket around the house.

"It won't be for much longer," Lacey told Percy one morning three weeks after Alvira and Sally had been secreted away. "Alvira is asking to come back to work."

"But you said she seemed happy," Percy answered.

"She is. She and Papa have struck up quite a friendship, but she wants to earn her own way. She enjoys my father's company and she doesn't want his pity. There's been no sign of Bert. Alvira is starting to think he gave up and went back south. She wants to come back to work."

"When?" Percy asked. She was anxious to have help again. The summer was pushing on and there was so much she wanted to do before the fall.

"I'll go get her on Thursday," Lacey promised.

"Three more days," Percy mused.

Lacey chuckled and left.

❧

Percy spent the rest of Monday and much of Tuesday planning out the work for the next several weeks. She could certainly make sure Alvira felt that she was earning her way. Tuesday's evening meal came. The men tousled their way through the line, eager for Percy's baked ham and scalloped potatoes. Taking delight in their pleasure, Percy stood behind the serving table and presided over the distribution of food. She made sure to fill a plate generously and set it aside for TJ, who was fetching firewood at his own insistence. He had undertaken the task every evening since his mother had left.

When the front door burst open unexpectedly, Percy jumped. A thick slice of ham slid off the serving fork and plopped to the floor. At the sight of the figure in the doorway, Percy felt herself become pale.

"Where is she?" demanded the roaring Bert Richards. "Where's my wife?" His soiled clothing bore witness to weeks of living in the woods. Dark angry eyes darted around the room.

"Ain't no wife here," Matt Harden returned fiercely. He glared at Bert defensively. "I don't know who you are and I don't much care, but Miss Morgan ain't anyone's wife."

"She's not the one I want." Bert lumbered toward the serving table. Percy inched backward involuntarily. "My wife was here. I know she was. Somebody here knows where she is. And I ain't leavin' until I find out where she and my girl went."

"I think you lost your trail, mister," Matt said, setting his half-filled plate down and turning toward Bert. "This is a lumber camp, not a refugee camp."

"I've been all over the backwoods of this state looking for my family. I believe I'll find them here. And you folks are going to help me or I'll give you a reason to help." Bert touched his hand to his hip and Percy saw the shape of what might be a pistol under his grimy clothing.

At the same moment, she heard shuffling in the kitchen. TJ! She heard the wood drop from his arms into the bin. Purposefully this time, she inched backward toward the door between the dining room and the kitchen. Under no circumstances must TJ come into the main room.

Matt stepped forward, accompanied by Carson Gregory. "Look, mister, whoever you are, this is by and large a peaceful place. We have our fights from time to time, but they're our own. We ain't looking to take on anyone else's."

Keep talking! Percy cried out in her mind as she moved slowly and quietly toward the kitchen. She heard TJ open the stove door and throw in a piece of wood. Next he would pump water to heat for washing dishes.

"I ain't askin' you to take on my fight," Bert Richards roared. "I'm just asking you to tell me where my wife and kids are."

At the door now, Percy leaned against it and pushed it open, slipping into the kitchen. She had no idea if Richards had noticed her. Swift action was the only alternative.

"TJ!" she whispered, taking his elbow and briskly guiding him toward the back door. He started to talk, but she silenced him with her finger to his lips. "Your father is in the dining hall. You have to get out of here. Go to Lacey's right now! Leave!" She literally pushed him out the back door and took a deep breath of relief as she saw him sprint around the side of the building toward the Gates house. She was tempted to sprint out after him, but if Bert noticed she was missing, there was no telling what he might do. TJ would go to Travis and Lacey, and help would be on the way. Bert was far outnumbered in the dining hall, but if he really had a gun, he would quickly have the advantage.

Quietly, her heart pounding, she slipped back into the dining room. As she surveyed the increasingly restless group, she was thankful for Lacey's wisdom in not telling anyone where Alvira and Sally had gone. Some of the men knew bits and pieces of her story and they knew she had fled an abusive husband. It was better for Alvira and the men that none of them could say where she was. Only Percy, out of fifty people in the room, knew the whereabouts of Bert's family and he was not going to find out from her.

"Where did you disappear to?" Bert demanded.

So he had noticed her absence.

"I was just checking on things in the kitchen," she answered evenly. Her voice sounded far more steady than she felt.

"Who's in the kitchen?" He lurched toward her, but Matt Harden stepped in his way. Bert pushed the smaller man aside, not easily, but successfully. Percy was backed up against the wall, Bert's face in hers. "If your mind is on the kitchen, then you don't realize the importance of my visit."

Percy did not answer.

"My guess is that you're in cahoots with that schoolteacher lady. You look like you'd be friendly with her."

Percy sucked in her breath and said nothing. Bert stank as if he had doused himself in whiskey.

"You gonna tell me where my woman is, or am I gonna have to give you some help?" He touched his hip again.

"I'll thank you to leave my dining hall," Percy said between gritted teeth. "You can see for yourself that your family is not here."

"You're gonna tell me where they are."

"No, I'm not."

"Yes, you are!" With a stealthy movement Percy would not have thought possible of someone so drunk, Bert reached into his pocket and pulled out a pistol.

"I will not be intimidated," Percy said insistently. "You will leave now or I'm sure some of these gentlemen will be happy to help you leave." She looked anxiously over her shoulder at Matt Harden and Carson Gregory. They were gesturing to each other, but they both caught her glance.

Bert Richards wheeled around, gun in hand. "I believe I have all the help I need," he said, waving the gun. "I promise you, it's loaded. Who's going to tell me where my family is?"

Percy looked around the room at the stone-faced men. They were not going to say a word, she could tell. Alvira's brief time among them had been enough to develop a protective layer of loyalty. But there was no reason any of them should be threatened for information they did not have.

"Don't bother with the men," Percy said. "They don't know where Alvira is."

"Ah, you know her name! So she was here!"

"It seems you've already ascertained that," Percy said briskly. "But she's not here now. So you might as well be on your way."

"I will be just as soon as you point me in the right direction."

"She's not going to point you anywhere," came a voice from the back of the room.

Josh! Percy turned to see Josh moving cautiously but steadily across the room. She had not even heard him come in, but his presence surely meant that TJ reached safety. Travis must not have been home or Josh would not have come alone, but surely he and Peter would appear soon.

Bert turned and leered at Josh. "You again. I thought you would have learned your lesson last time. You wanna get hurt again?"

Again? Percy thought, gasping inwardly. Had Josh hidden from her that Bert had hurt him the last time he stormed into town?

Josh put out his hand and continued walking toward Bert. "Give me the gun, Bert. Hurting somebody is not going to help anything."

"You all seem quite happy to steal my wife away. Don't you think that hurts me?"

"I'm sure it hurts," Josh said gently. Percy believed he really meant what he said. "It's not easy to have your life turned inside out. Let's put the gun away and talk this through."

Percy held her breath. No one else in the room made a sound as Josh reached out for the gun.

With a jerk, Bert moved the gun from Percy to Josh's face. Josh's chin pointed up as he moved it away from the pistol. He was frozen in place.

"I'm done sweet-talkin'," Bert growled. "If you think I won't shoot this thing, you got a lot to learn." He cocked the trigger.

Percy's heart leaped into her throat. Josh! She had treated him so brusquely in all his attempts to reach out to her. As much as she regretted her curt demeanor, she never seemed able to help herself. Suddenly she wanted to start fresh, to make things right with Joshua Wells, to receive the good intentions that he offered her. *It can't end like this!* she cried out silently.

"Dr. Wells does not know where your family is," Percy said abruptly. "I told you, I am the only one who knows."

The gun turned back toward her. Percy breathed deeply. No matter what happened to her, she would not let Josh be hurt if there was anything she could do about it.

"Then you talk to me!" Bert shouted. "If you care about your friend, you'll start talking!"

Percy glanced at Josh, who shook his head almost imperceptibly. That was all the encouragement she needed. Instantly, inexplicably, she trusted his gesture. "You'll get no help from me of any kind," she said firmly.

The gun swung back toward Josh. At the same moment, Carson Gregory and Matt Harden lunged at Bert from behind.

twenty-four

Instinctively, Percy's eyes squeezed shut. If Josh was to be shot, she could not bear to watch. She believed with every ounce of her being that Bert Richards was capable of pulling the trigger on that gun without remorse or pity. She had no idea what he was like when he was sober, and that did not matter much at the moment, for he was roaring drunk and angrier than she thought humanly possible. For a fleeting second she wanted to cry out that she would reveal Alvira's whereabouts to save Josh from further danger. But even if she had chosen to, the opportunity vanished instantly.

The combined weight of Matt and Carson and their precision in moving together gave Bert Richards no time to anticipate their action. Instead of a gunshot, Percy heard the thud as Carson and Matt knocked Bert Richards to the floor. Men all over the dining hall, freed from the paralysis that a cocked and pointed gun brings, pushed back their chairs and sprang to their feet.

Richards cursed loudly and thrashed against his attackers. Despite their momentary advantage, he would not be subdued easily. Percy forced her eyes open to see that he still waved the pistol in one hand. He gripped it, ready to shoot. Bert Richards was a strong man, more determined than ever in his drunken rage. One enormous boot kicked at Carson's head as Carson tried to restrain Bert's feet. Carson ducked the blows and persisted, clamping his hands down first on one ankle and then the other. Bert swung the pistol around Matt's head, somehow managing to keep a fraction of an inch ahead of Matt's grasping hands. To avoid a vicious blow to the jaw, Matt leaned backward, off balance. With a mighty one-armed jolt to Matt's chest, Bert sent the smaller man sprawling. Cursing continuously, Bert leered at Carson Gregory, still struggling to hold down his feet. Richards had gained the advantage he sought and Percy saw the monstrous contortion that his face took on and she was frightened all the more. Strength surged through his arms as he pointed the gun at Carson's face. Once again her eyes narrowed in anticipation of the gunshot.

From behind Bert, Josh threw himself at the big man and thrust his hands down on Bert's shoulders. His smaller size was no match for Bert's powerful torso and the two were soon entangled in a twisting wrestling match. Carson hung onto Bert's feet, but that did not stop Bert from rolling forcefully to one side. Ignoring his own pain, Matt scrambled to his feet and lurched toward Bert again. He joined the rolling fray, heedless of where the gun was now. Out of the side of her eyes, Percy could see a couple of other men moving in to help, but they could not cross the room quickly enough. Percy's common sense somehow overcame the urge to leap onto the tangled heap of men herself. If anything happened to Josh because she had kept silent about Alvira—she did not know if she could bear the thought.

Bert continued to threaten randomly with the gun. He needed no further provocation to pull the trigger, only the opportunity for a clear shot. The gun moved toward Josh's face. Carson Gregory shifted his position for a better grip. For a moment, Percy could not see Bert or Josh and in that moment, the gun went off.

For an eternity of a second, the room was motionless.

Unimaginable scenarios flooded Percy's mind. Common sense failing her now, she pitched forward toward the tangle of arms and legs that was Josh, Bert, Matt, and Carson. She could not see Josh, but the sudden stillness was ghastly. Slowly, far too slowly for Percy's liking, the men peeled themselves apart.

First, Carson released his fought-for hold on Bert's ankles, stood up, and backed away. As he did, he shook his head at the sight before him.

"What happened?" Percy cried out.

As Carson stepped away, Matt pulled himself to his knees, breathing heavily. His eyes did not move from the scene before him.

Percy had reached them now and she forced herself between Carson and Matt. Josh was up on his knees, finally, bent over Bert with blood soaking the front of his shirt.

"Josh!" Percy gasped. "You're hurt!"

He shook his head and rocked back on his heels. "Not me. Him."

Percy blanched as she saw the blood spurting out of Bert's chest.

"Somebody clear off a table," Josh barked. "We have to get him up where I can see what I'm doing."

"You're not going to try to save this piece of trash!" Carson shouted, incredulous.

"I'm a doctor. This is what I do." Josh's answer was firm. "What you do is up to you."

Carson stood frozen in his place as Josh pulled open the front of Bert Richards's shirt. "Clear a table!" Josh repeated urgently.

Behind her, Percy heard men rapidly swiping dishes off the nearest long table and scraping chairs out of the way. They heaved the table toward the spot where Bert Richards had been transformed from intruder to patient. Josh had one hand tucked under Bert's back and was leaning over with his ear to the big man's mouth, listening for breath.

"He's still breathing," Josh finally announced, "but I can't find an exit wound. I don't think the bullet came out."

"What does that mean?" Percy asked.

"It means we have to go in looking for it." He caught her eyes. "Sorry, but it looks like we'll have to commandeer your dining hall again for a temporary medical facility."

Several men, including Matt Harden, stepped forward and together they hoisted Bert Richards's limp form to the table. Josh immediately turned him on his side for a better look at his back, peeling off patches of bloodied clothing along the way.

"Did you find an exit wound?" Percy asked, wanting to know but hardly able to look for herself.

Josh continued to probe Bert's back. Finally he shook his head and rolled Bert to his back. "Definitely not. It went in here," he said, pointing to the hole in Bert's chest. "Based on the angle of the entry wound and the way the blood is spurting, I believe the bullet may be near the heart."

"So what do you have to do?"

"I'm going in."

"Going in?"

"It's his only chance."

"Are you talking about operating? Here? Now?"

Josh looked at Percy steadily and spoke quietly. "Yes. That is exactly what I'm talking about. And I need you to help. Will you?"

Stunned, she nodded mutely.

"My medical bag is over by the door. Can you get it? Then see about getting rid of the onlookers. I'm sorry about their supper, but I can't have everyone loitering around while I work."

"Yes, of course," Percy said, moving toward the door to scoop up the black medical bag. She whispered some instructions to Matt and Carson, gesturing toward the food and the kitchen. As she turned back to Josh, she could see the men organizing themselves to bring some order back to the dining hall.

"There are some scissors in there," Josh said.

"I remember," Percy responded, reaching into the bag and pulling out the scissors Josh had used to cut away Troy Wilger's dungarees all those weeks ago. Now, without being asked, she used them to remove what remained of Bert Richards's shirt. Blood pumped out as fast as she could sop it up with the few rags that were in the bag. Percy slipped off her apron and laid it across Bert's chest. It turned a deep purple almost immediately. She looked at his ashen face. Under other circumstances it would be possible to believe that he was an ordinary patient, an ordinary man with a family who had succumbed to an accident and needed a doctor. At a moment of need, Bert Richards looked like anyone else.

"The blood just keeps coming," Percy murmured as she rearranged her apron to absorb more.

Josh removed a scalpel from the bag and positioned it between his thumb and forefinger.

"Are you sure about this?" Percy asked, half under her breath.

Josh was breathing rapidly. "I took some surgical training. I admit I don't have a lot of experience, but I had a case like this once." He glanced at her. "Are you all right? You look pale."

"You don't look so well yourself," she said gently, "but if you're ready, I'm ready."

"Here we go." And with that, Josh made the incision and soon had his hand deep in Bert Richards's chest.

"What are you looking for?" Percy asked.

"We have to stop the bleeding. The bullet must have hit an artery."

"Can you sew up an artery?"

"I can try."

Josh worked by touch, not able to see but moving his hand around gently inside Bert's chest.

"I need more rags," Percy said. "I'll get them."

Her hands and dress bloodied, she ran to the kitchen. Some of the men were still pressed against the walls of the big room and a few had gathered in the kitchen. Percy ignored their inquiring looks and focused on her task. She retrieved a stack of dish towels and dashed back to Josh. Bert looked noticeably worse. Blood dribbled down the side of the table and pooled on the floor. Josh was visibly agitated.

"Is he. . .?" Percy started to ask.

Josh shook his head. "I think we're losing him."

twenty-five

They did lose him. Bert Richards expired on a wooden table in the dining hall on a muggy midsummer Tuesday night. The blood loss was rapid and voluminous, and it was only minutes after the gunshot when his heart stopped beating. Joshua Wells pulled his hand out of the man's chest and stepped back from the table. He opened his fist to show that he had indeed found the bullet, seconds too late. Percy lifted her eyes to meet his as they filled with the grief of a lost battle and a lost life.

"He's gone," Josh murmured. "I wanted to help him."

"You did everything you could." Percy reached out and grasped Josh's arm at the elbow. They were both sodden with the blood of Bert Richards. "You tried to save him. I'm not sure anyone else here would have done that. Besides, if he hadn't come in here with that gun. . . "

Josh shook his head slowly. "I know what you're thinking. . . that he deserved this. He was a wicked man and deserved what happened to him. But don't we all? Even when we bring things on ourselves we can hope that by the grace of God mercy will prevail."

Percy raised an eyebrow at such a philosophical response at this burning moment. She was fleetingly reminded of the time Josh had compared her to the wickedness of Troy Wilger. But this was not the time to pursue a theological discussion. Instead, she put her arms around Joshua Wells, whom moments earlier she had feared losing, and she breathed relief that he was not the man on the table.

Josh returned the embrace. "Thank you for helping," he murmured into her ear. "It was the only chance he had."

"And you were willing to give it to him."

Suddenly self-conscious, Percy glanced over her shoulder

at the row of men pressed against the far wall. Most of the men had scattered as soon as Bert was hoisted onto a table and Josh extracted a shiny scalpel from his bag. But a few had stayed to witness Josh cut open Bert's chest and plunge his hand inside. The men were pale now, one or two slumped into chairs. They were too busy holding onto their stomachs to notice her embrace with Josh.

The front door opened. Travis and Peter burst in, then stopped in their tracks. "What happened in here?" Travis demanded.

Josh pulled away from Percy and gestured weakly toward the table. Percy realized how rapidly the entire incident had happened. When she sent TJ off to safety, she expected Travis and Peter would come right away. And they had. But those few minutes had been enough to bring tragedy. Haltingly and briefly, she explained what had happened.

Josh sighed. "I'm glad you're here. We'd better move him and clean up."

"I'll heat some water," Percy mumbled and turned numbly toward the kitchen. Percy, Josh, Travis, Peter, and a small crew of men worked long into the night, erasing any clue of what had transpired.

The community was stunned. Fistfights broke out occasionally, and the danger of an accident with the machinery or lumber loomed over them always. But never in the camp's short history had a stranger thundered into town wielding a gun and then ending up with a sheet over his face.

⁂

In the morning, Travis went to fetch Alvira and Sally, bearing the mixed news that they were safe but at the expense of Bert's life. Their return to the camp, although a day earlier than planned, was somber. TJ held his mother and sister tightly as they sobbed, their shoulders racking with relief that their flight to freedom had come to its destination and sorrow that any glimmer of hope for restoration was now gone. That afternoon, Bert was buried quietly and unceremoniously in the first grave adjacent to the camp land. TJ refused to be present; and as soon as the last shovel of dirt was thrown over the hastily made pine coffin, Sally ran sobbing back to the shed she shared with her mother.

Percy walked with Alvira from the unmarked grave back toward the camp. "I never wished him dead," Alvira said.

"No one would blame you if you had," Percy said softly, remembering that more than once she had pondered that it would have been better if her own father had died than to do what he had done. She might still be with Ashley and their mother might have survived widowhood with more grace than she had brought to the shameful events they had endured.

"He was my husband and I once loved him. I wasn't always afraid of him. But he changed. It was like the demons got hold of him and he turned into someone I didn't know. But I never wished him dead, not ever, not a single time."

Percy put her arm around Alvira's shoulders. "I'm sure you didn't. That would not be your nature."

"I know folks thought I should stop putting up with him years ago. Miss Lacey thought that when TJ was just eight and she saw what was happening to him. I'm sure she thought I was weak, and I was."

Percy squeezed Alvira's shoulder. "No one is judging you now. You don't need to judge yourself so harshly."

If only she had learned that lesson herself. Not a day went by that Percy did not wonder what she could have done differently, any small thing that might have spared Ashley's being sent away.

Alvira sighed deeply. "Well, he is dead now and I'm not sure I'm sorry about that. I'm supposin' that makes me a horrible person, just as bad as he was."

"Alvira, don't. What you're feeling is normal; it's understandable. He treated you dreadfully."

"But I shouldn't be glad he's gone."

"You should be glad that you're safe now and your children are safe."

"Runnin' and hidin' all the time is no way to live," Alvira murmured.

"No, you're right about that." Percy had had her share of running and hiding. She wanted to be finished, but she knew she was not.

The camp is the best hiding place I've found, she thought, but lately she had more and more trouble hiding from herself, much less anyone else.

❧

Daniel Wells was waiting at his daughter's house when Percy and Alvira returned to the row of buildings. He looked gently upon Alvira and opened his arms to her. Unmindful of the roomful of people, Alvira walked directly to Daniel and received his embrace. He held her tightly as she buried her head in his shoulder.

Percy glanced at Josh, who in turn glanced at Lacey.

Alvira returned to working with Percy in the dining hall and took charge of the garden once again. But now, instead of working every waking moment of the day, she accepted an occasional afternoon off. She wanted to be free to see Daniel when he came to see Lacey, which now seemed to be at least once a week, sometimes more. Little time passed before Lacey, Josh, and Percy realized that it was not his children that Daniel came to see. After a perfunctory game of checkers with Adam or a lunch with Lacey, Daniel seemed to prefer a long afternoon stroll with Alvira.

One day Lacey insisted that Alvira and Percy join them all for lunch. Percy could see for herself the looks exchanged between Daniel and Alvira. When Lacey rose to clear dishes and carry them into the kitchen, Percy sprang up to help her; Josh was right on their heels.

"Did you see that, Lace?" Josh asked.

"You mean the way his eyes look?" Lacey responded.

Josh nodded. "He hasn't had that light in his eyes—"

"In eight years." Lacey finished her brother's thought. "Not since Mama got sick."

"What do you think this means?" Percy asked.

Lacey laughed. "You might not have your kitchen help for much longer."

Josh nodded. "Papa probably never thought about marrying again. He would never have gone looking."

"But when God puts someone in your path the way He put Alvira at the lighthouse," Lacey said, "it's hard to ignore."

The door between the dining room and kitchen opened. Daniel stuck his head in. "You're talking about me, aren't you?"

The trio looked shocked, then burst out laughing. "Yes, we were, Papa," Lacey finally said.

"I thought so. You should have been back long ago for more dishes. Come back in here and I'll give you something to talk about."

They regrouped around the table, joining Travis, the boys, Sally, and Alvira, who looked strangely nervous.

Daniel took Alvira's hand. "When the minister comes again," he said simply, "we want to have a ceremony. Nothing fancy, so don't outdo yourself, Lacey. After that, Alvira and Sally will move to the lighthouse."

"Papa!" Lacey exclaimed. "How wonderful!" She kissed her father's cheek and embraced Alvira. "Does TJ know?"

Daniel nodded. "He gave his blessing last week."

"Miss Lacey," Sally said, "does this make you my sister?"

Lacey grinned. "I suppose it does, in a way. I always wanted a sister."

The smile on Percy's face was sincere, if strained. What she had hoped for had come true. Alvira's story would have a happy ending. She would be cared for and treasured as she deserved. It was Percy's own story that strained the smile. Could anything turn her story around?

"Percy?" Suddenly she heard Josh's voice piercing through the resounding congratulations. "Are you all right?" His brown eyes, guileless and clear, held her, even from across the table; he was asking because he truly wanted to know.

She choked and said, "Yes, of course."

twenty-six

Josh moved toward Percy. "I'm afraid I don't believe you," he said softly. No one else heard what he said. "You don't look yourself."

She shrugged. "It's the announcement. Alvira is going to marry your father and move to the lighthouse. It will be hard to find someone to replace her."

Josh raised an eyebrow, skeptical. Percy ignored him. Plastering a smile on her face, she hugged Alvira and Daniel enthusiastically.

"I'm very happy for both of you," she said lightly. And she did mean it, despite what Joshua might think. "But I'm afraid I'm going to have to cut short my celebrating. I have some things I must do before supper."

"I should be helping you," Alvira said.

"No, no," Percy countered. "You stay and enjoy your afternoon. Come back to work when you're ready."

After a quick round of farewells, Percy successfully excused herself, but she did not head back to the dining hall. Instead, she stumbled into the woods behind Lacey's house. Sobs welled up inside her, unsubsiding, relentless. Racing against the rising force, she hurried her footsteps. Percy Morgan wanted to be far away from anyone else when the dam burst. Weeks, months, even years of grief pressed against the controlled facade she had erected and lived within. She tramped into the forest, mindless of where she went, not seeing the chipmunks that used to startle her with their scampering or the spreading tree roots that threatened to trip her. Putting one foot in front of the other more and more rapidly, she pressed on blindly.

At last she fell to the ground, exhausted, and gave way to

the tidal wave within her. Her shoulders heaved with her sobbing and the torrent that came from her eyes spilled down her face and splashed the ground beneath her. The sounds that came from her mouth were foreign to her. Not in five tumultuous years had she allowed herself such release, such protest, such catharsis. Percy lay flat on the ground, her head buried in her hands. It mattered not that the light beige of her dress became layered with black earth. Percy was not thinking of the moment when she would have to pick herself up and return to camp to prepare an evening meal. At the moment, she hardly thought it possible that she could do so. It seemed more likely that she would rise and circle around the camp and keep on walking till her feet carried her far away from this place where the truth was so unendurably present.

She did not hear the footsteps behind her. When he spoke her name, she raised her head awkwardly and looked around. "Joshua!"

"Yes, it's me. I told you I didn't believe you."

Percy sat up and began wiping tears from her cheeks with the back of one hand. She was unable to speak.

Josh sat in the dirt beside her and opened his arms. Without even the slightest hesitation, Percy allowed herself to fall against his chest. With his arms around her, he stroked her black hair with one hand. Josh said nothing for the longest time. He simply held Percy as she shivered with grief. Gradually, the tears subsided, the shaking dissipated, and Percy began to feel composed. She pulled herself upright, out of his embrace.

"I'm sorry," she said. "I don't usually. . .it's just that. . . well. . ." An explanation for her uncharacteristic lack of control seemed impossible. She returned to wiping tears off her face.

Josh smiled gently. "As fond as I am of Alvira, somehow I think this has a greater cause than just the loss of your kitchen assistant."

Percy sighed heavily. "It's a long story."

Josh shrugged. "I have time. I have a feeling it would do you good to tell your story."

Percy pulled her knees up under her chin and wrapped her arms around them. "I've never told it before. I'm not sure where to begin." She could hardly believe she heard herself speak those words, so contrary to her resolve that her past would not get in the way of her future.

Josh stretched his legs out in front of him and leaned back on one elbow. "How about if you start with why you know a lot about hand-carved European crown moldings but not so much about ordinary vegetable gardens."

Now Percy laughed through her tears. "It's just that while I was growing up, we had a lot of crown moldings, but I never saw where the vegetables came from. The cook brought them in, I suppose."

"The cook?"

"Yes, we had a cook and two maids and a gardener who looked after my mother's exotic idea of a garden."

"Two maids and a gardener?" Josh echoed.

Percy nodded. "And of course there was always a governess about the place, lest my sister and I run off to some corner of the house where we were not permitted to play."

"I didn't know you had a sister."

A cloud washed across Percy's face. "I did have one. I'm not sure if I still do or if she would want to acknowledge being related to me after all these years."

"How many years?"

"Five. Almost six."

Josh waited patiently for Percy to continue. For a fleeting moment, she considered cutting the conversation short and jumping up to lead the way back to the mess hall. After all, she still had an evening meal to prepare. But Josh's shining brown eyes cut through her resolve. With a sigh, she plunged in.

"I grew up in Connecticut. At the time I didn't know it, but we were quite wealthy. My friends all had the same standard of living. As a child, I didn't know anything different."

"What did your father do to earn such an income?"

"He was a banker. The president of a bank, actually. He worked all the time. We hardly saw him. I think that was part of why my mother was so withdrawn. She placed far more value on those flowers of hers than they were worth. I can see that now. She just needed something to devote herself to, since my father did not seem to care if she was around. Mother always talked about how she had failed to give him a son, as if that might have made things different. Some of the money was Mother's, actually. She had inherited a tidy sum when they married. Her family has had money for generations. The Percy name had to be steadfastly upheld by money."

"Percy is a family name?"

Percy nodded. "My mother's maiden name. I think I was supposed to be a boy to carry on both the Percy and the Morgan names. I disappointed them both from the start. Anyway, the money was Mother's, but she trusted Father implicitly. As soon as they were married, she signed everything over to him and never gave it another thought.

"Then one day Father announced he had to go to Chicago on bank business. He did that from time to time, so it was not unusual. But this time he did not come back. Mother waited weeks for word from him, and none ever came. We found out what he had done from another bank officer."

"What had he done?" Josh queried.

"He had been embezzling bank funds for years, more than a decade. He did have a meeting set up in Chicago, but he never got there. He just disappeared with all of Mother's money and hundreds of thousands that he had taken from the bank. It wasn't until after he disappeared that anyone really studied the books he kept. He had also mortgaged the house, which was my mother's. It was the Percy family home, and he mortgaged it heavily, then left town with the money. The bank foreclosed almost immediately. Mother had no way to repay the loan, of course. There was nothing left in their account. Father had taken it all, every penny. We had to move out, but we did not really have any place to go."

"Where did you end up?"

"My mother had a second cousin, Louise. They had known each other when they were little but had not been close as adults. Mother never really liked Louise, but what were we to do? We moved to New Jersey to live with Louise."

"Something must have happened there, or you would not have ended up here," Josh said, prodding her to keep going with her story.

"Mother was simply too frail. She hated that we had to go to Louise, and while Louise did take us in, she was none too happy about it. She never let a day go by without reminding Mother what a scoundrel she had married. Mother just started to disappear. At first she claimed exhaustion from the ordeal and wanted to rest for hours at a time between meals. Then she started coming out of her room only in the late afternoon. Eventually she did not come out at all, not even for meals. My little sister, Ashley, and I took food in to her and pleaded with her to eat. We wanted so much for her to get better and to stand up to Louise. But she never did. She just grew weaker and weaker every day until one morning she did not wake up. I'll never forget Ashley's scream."

"Ashley found her?"

Percy nodded.

"How old was she?"

"Seven. A seven-year-old girl should not wake up to find her mother dead."

"No, surely not," Josh agreed.

"After Mother died, Louise was even more irritated with me. I look a great deal like my father, and she blamed me for his actions."

"That hardly seems fair."

"Nevertheless, that is what happened. Louise found a boarding school somewhere in the Midwest and shipped Ashley off one day while I was out of the house. She wouldn't tell me where."

"That must have been awful!"

"It was. I begged and begged to know. She insisted it was for Ashley's own good, that the only way to save Ashley was to separate her from the Morgan family completely. But I was sixteen, nearly grown. I suppose Louise thought it was too late to redeem me. She simply said that I would have to leave."

"She threw you out?"

Percy nodded. "She gave me one week to make some plans, then told me I was on my own. She gave me enough money for room and board for about a month."

"And you've been on your own ever since."

"I gave her money back. Just left it on the doorstep one day. She hated me. I didn't want to touch her money."

"I can understand."

"I got a job washing dishes in a restaurant. It seemed to be the only skill I had. I hadn't been raised to actually work for a living, after all. I was supposed to marry into another rich family, multiply the family fortune, and live happily ever after. But after what happened, the young men who used to come calling didn't even want to mention my name."

"So how did you learn to cook?"

"By watching in the restaurant while I washed dishes. I didn't care what work I did. I only wanted to find Ashley. I knew she was somewhere in the Midwest. I thought perhaps she was in Chicago. All I know is that the school was called Miss Bowman's School for Girls."

"That isn't a lot to go on."

"No, it isn't. I never found Ashley. I worked in one restaurant after another in Pennsylvania and Ohio, just trying to keep moving west. Finally in Indiana I applied for a job as a cook, rather than washing dishes. They didn't ask for references. They only watched me cook. I got the job. And you know the rest after that."

"What about Ashley?"

Percy shrugged. "I never found her. I wish I could, but I don't think I can. Louise sends all my letters back unanswered."

Josh looked puzzled. "You're not likely to find Ashley way up here. So why did you come?"

The tears began again, slowly. "I've given up," she whispered hoarsely. "I can only hope she's happy. She's almost thirteen now. Perhaps she found someone at the school who would really care for her. And I hope deep in my heart that she knows I had nothing to do with banishing her."

"I'm sure she does. You must not give up hope, Percy."

A tear slipped off Percy's face and dribbled down her collar. "I hoped for as long as I could. I can't anymore."

Josh reached for her and took her in his arms again. "When you are weak and powerless, that is when God is strong and mighty. You must not give up hope, but you must hope in the right thing."

"I don't know what the right thing is anymore."

"When TJ was eight years old, Lacey told him that he was God's business. Look how that sustained him. You're God's business, Percy Morgan. He sent me here today just as surely as He sent Lacey into TJ's life all those years ago. You must always hope. And we will find Ashley."

twenty-seven

When Percy awoke the next morning, she could hardly believe what had happened in the forest with Joshua. As her mind moved into its morning mode, rising to awareness of the day's tasks, her pulse quickened at the implications of what she had done. No longer could she hide behind a facade of competence. No longer could she insist that she was fine to his probing eyes and expect that he should believe her.

Unexpectedly, relief washed over her. She got out of bed, reached automatically for her gray work dress, and began to dress. On the floor in a heap was the beige dress she had worn the day before, soiled with the forest earth. Percy stooped and picked it up. She fingered the hem, which had trailed in the dirt for miles until it was black, and reflected on her flight. Running from Daniel and Alvira's happiness had been an irresistible impulse, an overwhelming wave that she could not contain. But after five long years of running, she was finished. Josh had gently turned her back toward camp, taking her hand in his as they retraced the rugged miles together. Now, on this morning, instead of waking with fear and regret, she relished the relief that someone, especially Josh, at last knew the truth.

After breakfast, Alvira insisted on cleaning up by herself and she shooed Percy out the door with instructions to relax and enjoy the morning. The impulse to protest was fleeting. Instead, Percy stepped outside into the sunshine and wandered aimlessly toward the garden. The green beans were doing well and there would be plenty of radishes and onions. She was anxious to know how well the carrots were growing and she fingered the lacy green topper of a plant at the edge of the patch. Would it hurt to pull up just one carrot to see how the whole row was faring?

"If you pull it up to see how big it is, you can't put it back."

Percy spun around to see Joshua standing, smiling, at the far end of the garden. "The carrot," he said, gesturing toward her fingers on the carrot top. "I used to pull them up to see how big they were getting. It made Mama mad, but I was so curious I couldn't help myself."

Percy smiled. "I assure you, I have no intention of doing any such thing."

"But you are curious, aren't you?" Josh walked slowly toward her between the tomatoes and the bean stalks.

"Yes, I confess I am. I want to know if there really are carrots under there."

"Mama always told me that I had to have more patience and give God time to do His work."

"I guess that's one way to look at it." *If you believe in God,* she added silently.

Josh sat in the dirt beside her. "Some things you just have to take on faith and wait."

"For how long?"

"Until it's time."

"And how will I know when it's time? I suppose Lacey will tell me when it's time to dig up the carrots."

"The carrots, yes. The other things you'll have to figure out by yourself."

Percy fell silent. Josh knew her whole story now. So Percy knew that he meant what he said.

Josh ran his fingers in the soil and let the dirt drizzle through his fingers. "I remember the day you rode into town, so to speak," he said, "with that crotchety carriage driver."

"Mr. Booker."

"Yes, Mr. Booker. I remember thinking that there was something remarkable about you right from the start. After all, you talked him into bringing you up here against his better judgment. After everything you told me last night, I think you are all the more remarkable."

"You do?" Percy looked up to catch his eye.

"Absolutely. You're determined, hardworking, resourceful, organized, and brave."

Percy had no response. Her heart beat faster at the thought that Joshua Wells thought she was all those things.

"Do you remember the night I walked you to Lacey's, after you were brave enough to help me with Troy?"

Percy nodded.

"We talked about the stars," Josh continued. "I remarked that the Maker of the Stars had been in your little bedroom that night, helping us care for Troy. I may think the world of you, Miss Percy Morgan, but what the Maker of the Stars feels about you is what really matters."

Percy pursed her lips. "As I recall, on that same night you also told me that I was just as much trouble as that wretched Troy Wilger."

"That's right. I did say that. None of us is really any different than Troy."

"How can you compare yourself to Troy Wilger?" Percy protested. "You risked your life when Bert Richards burst into the dining hall. You tried to save Bert's life when the others were ready to leave him to die. Troy wouldn't have done that."

"No, probably not," Josh agreed. "But Troy doesn't look at the stars much. He doesn't know the Maker. That's the real difference."

Percy was silent for a long time. She remembered the well-thumbed Bible she had seen on Joshua's nightstand that night. At last she said, "And you do know the Maker?"

He nodded. "When I look at those stars, I don't just see their light. I see the One who gave them light. And that's who was in that room with us that night with Troy, and at that table in the dining room with Bert. And in the forest with you last night."

Percy sniffled and held back her tears.

"The Maker sent me to you last night," Josh said, "just as

He sent Lacey to TJ and Alvira eight years ago. You've been afraid I would turn my back on you if I knew the truth, haven't you?"

Percy nodded. "Everyone else has," she croaked. "I'm sorry for all the times I rebuffed you. I knew you were trying to be my friend. It's just been so long since anyone did that for me. I didn't know what to do."

Josh shook his head. "Your father failed you, Percy. Your cousin, Louise, failed you. Your friends failed you when you needed them most. But not the Maker. It's understandable that you would hesitate to trust other people to care for you. You've had to look out for yourself all these years. But the Maker of the Stars is on your side, Percy Morgan. You haven't tried depending on Him." Josh put his hand on a carrot top. "I believe there is a carrot growing in the ground under this. And so do you, or you wouldn't be tempted to dig it out early. Some things you take on faith."

"You say that so easily."

He shrugged. "I'm preaching far more than I meant to. But when I saw you hovering over the carrots with that hopeful look on your face, I couldn't help myself." Josh stood up and brushed the dirt off his trousers.

Percy squinted up at him. "Did you and Alvira plan this?"

"What do you mean?"

"She practically chased me out of the kitchen, as if I was going to be late for an appointment, and almost as soon as I sat down here, you came along with your little sermon."

Josh's brown eyes twinkled. "No, Alvira and I did not plan this. Someone else did." He turned and strolled away, hands leisurely in his pockets.

Percy watched him walk away. Once again, relief washed over her.

twenty-eight

The garden gave a good harvest. Percy learned to can. The cellar was stocked for the winter. And Alvira prepared for her wedding.

As the summer sun burned through July and August, Percy labored in the heat of the day and sought refreshment in the cooler air that came with nightfall. Her garden became a favorite spot, because it was out in the open, away from trees or structures. From the carrot patch, she could easily see the night sky. Resolutely, she resisted the temptation to check on the carrots' growth. Lying on her back in the garden, against the cool earth, sometimes with Josh next to her, she dared not even try to count the stars she had not noticed during the spring and early summer. Caught up in work and anguish, she had not raised her eyes often to the gemmed, sparkling field of black in those weeks. Now she often would stare at the stars, wondering, was the Maker of the Stars looking back at her?

When she pondered Joshua's growing companionship, which she no longer rebuffed, Percy celebrated a gift. A gift of friendship; a gift of confidence; a gift of faith and hope. Laughter, not the cautious sort but free laughter, returned to her face. Her grandmother's Bible had been promoted from the bottom of the trunk to the bedside table. A great deal of what she read still puzzled her, but she continued to read.

Still, she ached for Ashley and kept herself from surrendering to happiness without word from her cousin, Louise. Joshua had carried through on his promise to help find Percy's sister. In the most official language he could muster, he had written to Louise, imploring her to reveal information about Ashley's whereabouts. When his letter was not immediately returned, as all of Percy's had been, Percy allowed herself a glimmer of hope. But the letter eventually was returned, unopened, by the postal service, with the notation that Louise was now deceased.

That night, Percy huddled in her room in blackness, the curtains drawn against the moonlight, the lamp extinguished, until Josh came to her to insist that they had not reached the end of the trail. There were other relatives, he said, and there must have been an attorney to settle Louise's estate. They would persist until they found Ashley. With his arms around her, he lifted her to her feet and led her outside to see the night sky. The Maker of the Stars, he repeated, had not abandoned her. She longed to believe.

ぶ

Daniel and Alvira chose to marry facing the western sky at sunset, in the meadow behind the lighthouse, on an early autumn evening. The visiting minister joined Peter and Joshua's dream of a church for the emerging town, but for now, the people would have to settle for his occasional visits for official acts.

Daniel and Alvira faced the minister, with Lacey and Travis, Peter and Abby, Josh and Percy, TJ, Sally, and Micah gathered around them. Abby's children squirmed some, but Adam and Caleb Gates were ecstatic about acquiring a grandmother, and they paid rapt attention to the brief service. The same minister had presided over the unions of Peter and Abby, and then Lacey and Travis two years after that.

Looking past the minister while he gave a brief homily, Percy's eyes wandered to the lighthouse. Against the glowing orange sky, it glimmered in the evening air with freshness and life. Daniel maintained an immaculate tower. Josh and Lacey had both told her stories of ships that had crashed around in dark, treacherous, winter waters below, depending on the light that came from the top of the tower to beckon them toward safety. Somehow she knew what those shipmasters must feel like—the anxious searching in the midst of a swirling storm, the unpredictable heavings of a craft powerless against the wind and waves. Would a small light at the top of a distant tower really be enough to guide the way to safety and calm sailing?

The minister said, "You may kiss the bride," and Daniel gladly complied.

Adam tugged on Alvira's skirt. "Are you my grandma now?"

She scooped him up. "I would be delighted to be your grandma." Caleb clamored into her embrace as well.

Percy felt Josh at her elbow. "It was a lovely ceremony," she murmured, "and a lovely time of day for it."

"Papa has always liked the sunset," Josh explained. "He knows that the darkness comes next, and says that should make us appreciate the gift of light all the more. I think finding Alvira after all these years alone, well, it's a new dawn for Papa, a new gift of light."

"Yes, a gift of light," she echoed softly. "The ships must feel that way about the lighthouse when they pass at night and the weather is bad."

"The trick is not to look at the weather, not to mind the darkness," Josh replied. "They have to watch the light at all times, keep it in their sight, aim toward it."

"I imagine the night can be very long out there."

"Yes, but the lighthouse is a beacon of safety and the dawn always comes."

"Yes, I suppose it does," Percy murmured. "If they make it through the night."

Josh paused. "You'll make it through your night, Percy. The dawn will come."

She looked at him, wordless, suddenly filled with belief. Perhaps he was, after all, right about the Maker of the Stars.

The small wedding entourage began making its way toward the house for cake and refreshments. Josh put his hand on Percy's elbow to guide her. "I talked to Peter about modifying the plans for the personal quarters behind the clinic," he said casually.

"Oh? But he hasn't even finished building the clinic yet."

"That's why I thought I should talk to him now," Josh

explained. "I want to add several more rooms—a proper kitchen, another bedroom, maybe even a dining room."

"That sounds more like a house than a clinic."

"Perhaps you're right. But I'm going to need more space, at least enough for two people to live in without falling all over each other. And I hope there will be children later."

She stopped in her steps and turned to stare at him.

"We can always add another story. I wonder if you would like to see the new floor plan."

"Me?"

"Yes, you. I was rather hoping that you would consent to being the other person living behind the clinic. Perhaps the next time the minister comes around, it will be our turn."

"Our turn?"

"To marry."

"Marry?"

"Yes." He took her hand in his. "Percy Morgan, will you marry me?"

She fell into his arms and only when she heard clapping did she realize that the others were listening.

"Does this mean the lady from the street is going to be my aunt?" Adam asked his mother.

Lacey grinned at Percy expectantly.

Percy smiled at Adam. "I would be delighted to be your aunt."

A Letter To Our Readers

Dear Reader:

In order that we might better contribute to your reading enjoyment, we would appreciate your taking a few minutes to respond to the following questions. We welcome your comments and read each form and letter we receive. When completed, please return to the following:

Rebecca Germany, Fiction Editor
Heartsong Presents
PO Box 719
Uhrichsville, Ohio 44683

1. Did you enjoy reading *Light Beckons the Dawn?*
    ☐ Very much. I would like to see more books
       by this author!
    ☐ Moderately
       I would have enjoyed it more if _____

    _____

    _____

2. Are you a member of **Heartsong Presents**? Yes ☐ No ☐
    If no, where did you purchase this book? _____

    _____

3. How would you rate, on a scale from 1 (poor) to 5 (superior), the cover design? _____

4. On a scale from 1 (poor) to 10 (superior), please rate the following elements.

    _____ Heroine   _____ Plot

    _____ Hero   _____ Inspirational theme

    _____ Setting   _____ Secondary characters

5. These characters were special because_____

_____

_____

6. How has this book inspired your life?_____

_____

_____

7. What settings would you like to see covered in future
   Heartsong Presents books?_____

_____

_____

8. What are some inspirational themes you would like to see
   treated in future books?_____

_____

_____

9. Would you be interested in reading other **Heartsong
   Presents** titles?   Yes ❑   No ❑

10. Please check your age range:
    ❑ Under 18   ❑ 18-24   ❑ 25-34
    ❑ 35-45   ❑ 46-55   ❑ Over 55

11. How many hours per week do you read?_____

Name _____

Occupation _____

Address _____

City _____ State _____ Zip _____

From her

home in Washington State, VeraLee Wiggins penned four complete novels of historical inspirational romance before going to her eternal reward. The long-awaited collection houses the beloved romance tales of Rachel Butler and Martha Lawford who met on the Oregon Trail and became the best of friends. In *Heartbreak Trail,* Rachel meets two men who vie for her heart. In *Martha My Own,* Martha is left on her own in a strange new land, contemplating a marriage proposal out of the necessity for survival. True love won't come for Martha until *Abram My Love.* Then *A New Love* tells the story of love fulfilled in both womens families and homes.

paperback, 464 pages, 5 ³⁄₁₆" x 8"

Heart♥ng Presents
Love Stories Are Rated G!

That's for godly, gratifying, and of course, great! If you love a thrilling love story, but don't appreciate the sordidness of some popular paperback romances, **Heartsong Presents** is for you. In fact, **Heartsong Presents** is the *only inspirational romance book club*, the only one featuring love stories where Christian faith is the primary ingredient in a marriage relationship.

Sign up today to receive your first set of four, never before published Christian romances. Send no money now; you will receive a bill with the first shipment. You may cancel at any time without obligation, and if you aren't completely satisfied with any selection, you may return the books for an immediate refund!

Imagine. . .four new romances every four weeks—two historical, two contemporary—with men and women like you who long to meet the one God has chosen as the love of their lives. . .all for the low price of $9.97 postpaid.

To join, simply complete the coupon below and mail to the address provided. **Heartsong Presents** romances are rated G for another reason: They'll arrive *Godspeed!*